PERSEPHONE IN HELL

C.F. Joyce

Westport River Publishing

PERSEPHONE IN HELL

Published by:
Westport River Publishing
Westport, Massachusetts

Copyright © 2014 by C.F. Joyce

This book is a work of fiction. Any references to historical events, real people, or real places are used fictitiously. Other names, characters, places, and events are products of the author's imagination, and any resemblance to actual events or places or persons living or dead is entirely coincidental.

All rights reserved, including the right to reproduce this book or portions thereof in any form whatsoever.

With special thanks to Marjorie Walsh for permission to use original artwork for cover, copyright © 2014.

ISBN-13: 978-0990427711   Westport River Publishing
ISBN-10: 0990427714

Library of Congress Control Number: 2014945374
Westport River Publishing, Westport Massachusetts

This story is dedicated to my family

Ma, Dad, Larry, Sara, Dinah, Jane, and David

Nannie and Sookie

Rob, Laura, and Greg

thank you for witnessing my life

A story of spring

In ancient times, it is said that Hades, brutal King of Hell, rose to earth and ripped the young innocent goddess Persephone from her fields and flowers. He dragged her to the underworld. Against her will, he made her his wife.

Demeter, Persephone's mother, was incensed. She flew to Zeus and demanded he negotiate Persephone's return to Olympus.

Zeus was the mightiest of all gods. He called Hades to account. But it was too late. For Persephone in her lonely desperation had eaten three pomegranate seeds from Hades' table. Unknowingly, she had bound herself to Hell for eternity.

Still, the King of Mount Olympus could not be denied, and Hades relented. He would free Persephone. For half each year, she could seed the fields and raise the greenness of earth with her loving mother Demeter. But when the harvest was over, she had no choice but to return to the underworld as Hades' wife, Queen of Hell.

Thus each year, our goddess Persephone brings the bounteous warmth of spring. And every winter, Demeter cries icy tears of despair while her daughter waits in Hell for a new beginning.

Persephone in Hell

THE MEMORIES

I recall years long gone, at least I think the memories are real. I remember wanting to be someone else, anyone else. I despised my name, my nickname even more, and the oak trees, the snow, and the cow town where I lived my tedious life. I'd have been queen of all England, but Massachusetts haunted me and wouldn't let me go.

How can I account for those days, those seminal moments, that ancient crucible of time? Forty years or more later, facts get confused. 1968 and 1969 — hallmark years; years filled with Vietnam and civil rights, with changing hemlines and women's liberation. Landing on the moon. An era of great upheaval, so it seemed, so all the papers proclaimed.

But of course so many things stay the same whether a teenage girl likes it or not. Mother Nature is cruel; she keeps us in our place, making us wait no matter how hard we fight her rule. Or she pushes us out, like baby birds too long in the nest. Her seasons vary — they change over and over again, but not really — they're always coming back. Spring returns. Mothers and daughters, sisters and best friends, families — nothing unique, nothing that hasn't come a hundred thousand times before.

How can I know what was real, what imagined; which pieces matter — what parts to discard? All I have are my twisted, broken remembrances of things past - my muddied collection of feelings, harsh and inharmonious, jubilant, mournful. They push at me; they cut through time. They come back to taunt me, they refuse to leave me alone. Over oceans of time, across that vast sea, I recall my glory days and wonder what Mother Nature could have been thinking; how savage my journey, my struggle to feel loved.

I didn't ask for it, didn't want it to be this way. Stories... memories choke my mind.

[Glory the Ancient]

MONDAY MORNING

It was the bleakest of mornings, a fine example of Mother Nature's often torturous cruelties. *What did I do to deserve this? Beastly frigid. Christ, it's cold.* Glory trudged down the snowy street in her platform shoes to school.

Bad enough it's Monday. I despise Mondays. Waking up at six a.m. on any day of the week is pitiless. But Mondays are downright abusive. It's still dark out. What kind of farmer do people think I am? I need my sleep.

The north wind showed no mercy. *The high school principal phoned Ma just last week. He said I called in sick seven Mondays in a row. The man is an idiot - it took him seven weeks to figure out the pattern.*

So now, it's goddamn six forty-five on a freezing cold Monday morning with Ma insisting on school.

Glory had pleaded with her mother, who got up especially early to make certain not to be fooled again. "Joyce," Glory begged, "you know I can't stand it. I hate going. Let me stay home."

It was the dawn of miseries. Even the goddess Aurora herself, pulling the sun through the heavens in her chariot of gold and red, couldn't have wished for that particular daybreak. And Glory's mother was in no mood for an argument. She gave her daughter the imperious look that meant don't even bother, and said calmly, "I'm your mother. Call me Ma."

Glory threw on her coat, wrapped her royal purple scarf around her neck, and huffed her way out the back door.

Joyce closed her eyes and leaned against the kitchen sink. Her daughter tried her patience more often than not, but she had to admire that spirit. You can't make Glory do anything she doesn't want to do, she thought. She turned and went back to her coffee.

Glory's a puzzle, Joyce continued in her mind. She may hate going to school. But she did indeed walk out the door. Hey, here's a theory! She must like being in school, if only a little. I'll figure the correlations. Joyce reveled in the mathematical logic of it all.

~~~~~~

Glory picked her way around the snow banks and ice puddles. The sidewalk across from the field hadn't been plowed. She walked on the edge of the street in the slush.

Dirty lumpy piles of it frozen everywhere. Whoever said snow is pretty, obviously never saw slush.

Her books were heavy, and it was a whole mile to school. Well, just under a mile. If the house had been a few blocks farther away, past the mile mark, Glory could have taken the school bus — easier, though not exactly the coolest way to arrive at school. *But no, they make me walk.*

The wind picked up, and Glory's thighs were turning red. She felt numb with chill. Her long dark hair, wild and frizzy, collected mist that froze as it clung to her curls. Her nose and eyes ran from the harsh wind, and as she wiped at her face with a frosty glove, Glory stepped squarely into a slush puddle. "Oh, crap! My shoes!" she yelped in pain as her toes hit the icy water.

For crying out loud. She glanced back and realized that she was out of sight of Ma and Mrs. Fournier, who lived in the house next door and was surely keeping an eye on the street for safety's sake. *Even at this ungodly hour.*

A truck appeared down the road. Glory stood in the street with her coat undone, flying in the wind. She stuck out her thumb. Within seconds she had a ride. She climbed awkwardly into the cab, her miniskirt hiking up. Her frozen legs refused to move quickly. "Where's a pretty girl like you goin'?" asked the trucker.

"Down the road a bit," she replied. The driver didn't know that Gloria always said exactly what she meant.

"Happy to take you with me, little lady," the man said, clearly pleased with his run of good luck. The truck pulled back into the street. The trucker glanced over and watched as Glory rubbed her bare red thighs.

I'm so damn cold. Will spring never come? She closed her eyes, willing Persephone, the goddess of spring, to arise from the dead. Nothing happened.

Should know better than to trust in the gods. Maybe I'll thumb my way to Florida.

Her fingers moved up and down her frigid skin, trying to create some heat. The trucker's hand left the steering wheel and inched across the vinyl seat toward her. "It's like ice in here," he said softly so as not to disturb her reverie. "I can help with that."

Glory gave up on the gods for the moment and stared out the steamed up window. She counted the side streets they slowly passed – Forest Street, Chestnut Street, Spring Hill Lane. *Such vernal, innocent places, green and natural. Merry and naked, nothing like winter; no snow drifts ever on Spring Hill.*

The truck came up on Sherwood Lane as the man's hunger searched for warmth in the girl sitting trance-like beside him.

I wonder if England had street names back in the days of Robin Hood and Maid Marion. That's stupid, I suppose there were no streets at all, just paths leading to the castle. Robin lived in the forest, idiot, not the town. You can't find your way through the forest, that's the whole point. You can disappear and only be found if you want to be.

Glory's intense violet eyes strained to see through the foggy glass. *Robin stopped hiding in Sherwood just long enough to save Maid Marion from being forced to marry the evil Sheriff of Nottingham. Where is Nottingham, anyway?*

And where was good King Richard when you needed him? Off to fight the silly Crusades. That's a man for you. You can't count on good winning out. You can't count on men being good. And you couldn't count on any man, not even a lionhearted king, to protect you from the slime bags of the world. No man but Robin, of course, and he isn't real. You can't keep a real man from forcing his way on you.

Several centuries and half a mile went by. Glory ended her day dream in time to spot Birchwood Street and told the driver, "Okay, you can stop now."

His excitement had built and he didn't want to let her go. "What are you talkin' about, honey? We're just gettin' started — I ain't stoppin' now."

"I have to get out. School's that way." She pointed left. "Can't be late, I'll get detention again."

He said, "I ain't lettin' you out. This is my truck. You'll play by my rules." He winked at her with an ugly slyness, his mouth curled up in a grin.

Disgusting creep. Her violet eyes lit the dawn and called the royalty within her to account. Like Aurora herself, she controlled the morn. She turned to him with the calm of an ancient queen. "No one tells me what to do. Certainly not a savage like you. Now let me out or Zeus may strike you dead."

The man's eyes widened in surprise and not a little regret. But he pulled over to the curb, and as he stopped, let out a belly whopper of a laugh. "You sure have spunk. You're a magnet for trouble," he said admiringly.

~~~~~~

Glory didn't have to hitch a ride the rest of the way. Mike drove by and picked her up. One of the few kids in school with a car, Mike was rich and owned a Mustang. But he seemed nice, not snobby, and didn't hold it against her that she was poor. The radio was playing, and Glory sang along. "I wanna hold..." She looked over at Mike, who seemed amused and a little embarrassed. Hmmm, he doesn't like the Beatles? Glory wondered. Who doesn't like the Beatles?

They made it to school by seven ten, fully ten minutes early. To date, this was Glory's best time for getting to school – one for the books. But she didn't stay in the parking lot with Mike. Instead, she hurried into school, waving to the principal as she rushed past him and into the nearest girls' room to check the damage to her mascara and lip gloss. *Must warm up. Winter is the pits.*

The principal shook his head as she flew by. "Gloria is impulsive – always in a rush," he told his assistant. "But at least I can count her present and on time today – and it's a Monday!"

~~~~~~

Glory didn't have much homework that night. The peewees were in bed. Dad always went to sleep early. And Penny and Sammy were in the dining room with their books spread out everywhere. Exams tomorrow. She waited up for her mother to come home from her shift.

Ma walked in the house and lit a cigarette. She stood at the kitchen table and wearily scrambled eggs for her late night supper.

"Ma," Glory wondered, "why don't you ever check up on me? I kind of thought you'd call the school to make sure I didn't skip today."

"It's been a long day, my dear," Ma said, remembering her six o'clock wake up. "And, no news is good news," she explained with a knowing look on her tired face.

Gloria didn't consider hitchhiking newsworthy. "I made record time," she responded proudly.

"That's my girl," Ma answered as she turned up the heat on her eggs.

Glory looked around the dirty kitchen. She saw dishes piled high in the sink, and a stovetop that no one ever cleaned encrusted with weeks' worth of cooking. *God, Sunday's papers, dumped in a corner on the linoleum floor.*

"Ma?" she wondered. "Have you ever wanted to be rich and famous, like a movie star? Have you ever wanted to be someone besides yourself?"

"Why do you ask?" Joyce answered.

"I hate my life."

Joyce chuckled. "That's a tad dramatic, don't you think?"

"Being me is so boring. A movie star has adoring fans. Everyone knows she's gorgeous, in the spotlight in Hollywood and Times Square. She might climb the Eiffel Tower or visit Stonehenge at the summer solstice. Or sail the Atlantic first class passage." Glory had never seen a real passenger ship. "A movie star plays lots of roles; she can pretend to be whoever she wants. I'll bet a movie star's life is always exciting."

Joyce wasn't so sure. She sighed. "Gloria my dear, life is unfair. What can I say? I suppose you'll just have to live with being you. It's not really so bad being you, is it?"

Glory answered without having to think. "I'd much rather be someone else. I don't even like my name. Gloria – it's such a stupid name, and "Glory" makes me sound like a baby. The only thing I like about me is my eyes. Everything else on the list - get rid of it, chop it off!" Glory laughed a deep Poobah laugh.

"But maybe a queen is a better choice than a movie star. Because a queen is real, not just pretty. She has power. And she can come and go as she pleases, and has loyal followers to do her bidding." Glory glanced around her filthy house. *Cobwebs up at the ceiling.*

"A queen doesn't have to live in a messy house. She could discover new worlds. Someday she might even fly to the moon on a rocket ship. If you could be a queen, Ma, who would you be?"

Glory's mother considered the exhausting day she had just finished. "I suppose Cleopatra," she replied. "Why? Cleopatra floated down the Nile on her own barge. She could be alone anytime she wanted. She made rules to suit herself."

Ma took a drag on her Chesterfield and flicked the ashes into the kitchen sink. "Oh, and she drank lovely coconut milk and ate figs dipped in honey. Egypt is hot but not ungodly humid like here in summer. She had the gentle breezes of the Nile to keep her cool. Yes, I'd be Cleopatra if I had a chance."

She scraped her scrambled eggs onto a plate and took a last drag of her cigarette. She looked for an empty ashtray. Every one of them overflowed. She dropped the butt into a coffee cup left on the table from breakfast. Joyce closed her eyes for a moment and luxuriated in the notion of being all alone. "Who would you be, Glory?"

"I know it's dumb, but I've got to get a new name, and I want the coolest name in the world. The best by far is Elizabeth, don't you think?

I want to be rich and famous, and powerful beyond all reason. And wicked beautiful, of course, and have cool clothes, something different to wear for every season of the year. I want to do good deeds for the people of my country. I must travel the world and see every corner of the British Isles. Search for Sherwood Forest and Camelot and the Hundred Acre Wood."

And attract handsome followers, naturally. Glory blushed.

"I'll be the great Queen Elizabeth, the First among all queens."

She smiled. It was an excellent choice, the choice of a lifetime. *It all makes sense. Though how I'll get myself to the moon, I'm not sure.*

Only the vast sea of time held that answer.

THE BREAD BOX

Glory slammed the kitchen drawer shut with a huge bang. "Why isn't there ever anything to eat around here?" she protested to no deity in particular. "Nothing in there but some old bread and Penny's warm apples."

Penny was Glory's older sister; the only one in the family who liked her apples at room temperature. Penny's front teeth were sensitive. She couldn't bite into a cold apple straight from the refrigerator bin – when she tried, she would get a painful shivering feeling that went all the way down her back. "For God's sake," Glory continued, "even the saltines are gone."

She opened the bread box again in hopes that she had missed something hiding among the ruins. She took a good look inside. There were a few pieces of dark, sour pumpernickel bread, a long loaf of spongy white bread, three badly bruised Macintosh apples, and a crushed box of graham crackers.

Lots of stale crumbs strewn on the bottom of the draw. Empty plastic packaging, but no coffee cake. No muffins. Christ, not even any decent crackers. No cookies, not even homemade.

Ma came home from the grocery store each Saturday with one box of store bought cookies. Glory and her five siblings considered store bought cookies highly superior, especially the Mallomars, delicious chocolate covered marshmallow treats. The box full was devoured within a day of purchase, sometimes within the hour it came home to the bread box.

With six kids in the family, you have to target a cookie if you want to hold onto it. *You have to stake your claim, like Sir Walter Raleigh, whose ships sailed all the way across the unknown sea, proclaiming the new world Virginia for his virgin queen Elizabeth. You have to stand by it so that no one else can eat it before you have a chance. It's serious business, marking your store bought cookie against the starving hordes.*

It was a consequence of little money and a large hungry family. Everyone competing for the same few crumbs.

She grabbed the white bread. *Cheap, off brand stuff. I hate being poor. Why can't we ever get Wonder Bread? Still, the only edible thing in the bread box.* She took out two slices and shoved the rest back in the drawer. She poured cinnamon over the bread, and sprinkled sugar on. *It will have to do,* Glory thought with an irritation she'd carried around all day.

She took a bite. *Food certainly not fit for a queen, not even for a knighted follower. True peasant fare perhaps, meant for sailors or even savages. Though to give the cinnamon sugar bread credit, it really is fairly tasty, better than old dented apples.*

I wonder if apples grow in Israel, it's awfully hot there. Maybe only Hebrew royalty ate apples if they were that precious. I wouldn't have been a queen. Well, possibly. Nannie's name is really Ester, and Ester was a queen. Maybe in a past life I was a Jewish queen. Glory, queen of the Hebrews. Hmmm, in this life I think I'll keep that to myself.

Glory might have been happy. It was February school vacation, and she was driving with Dad the next morning into Boston to stay at Nannie and Aunt Sadie's house. She'd be there for the whole week. It was a tradition. She went in February; Penny during April school vacation. It was a way to get the kids out of their cow town and back to civilization, if only temporarily.

Sammy, Penny's twin brother, wasn't invited anymore. The last time he stayed with his grandmother and aunt, when he was twelve, he'd knocked over a lamp in the living room. Sammy had cried and apologized. "Boys will be boys," Ma said to her sister.

But Sadie was furious. She remembered the Depression when she was terribly poor, when they had nothing. She never had nice things, she told Sammy. "That lamp came all the way from Japan. You've gone and broken my beautiful porcelain oriental table lamp," she said. She wouldn't let Sammy forget it.

"It's alright," Ma said to Sammy afterwards. "It wasn't so awful what you did. I know you didn't mean it. Aunt Sadie has been through a lot. She'll never forget you broke her lamp. But let's just pretend it didn't happen. Besides, you have more fun at home where there's plenty of room to stretch and run. It's good we moved across from the field."

Ma smiled at Sammy, her first born along with Penny of course. He's such a precocious child, she thought. So bright, so smart. Why she valued her boys over her girls, she herself didn't understand. But there it was. Sammy was the light of her life. He could do nothing wrong.

~~~~~~

I hate this house. I can't wait to get away.

Glory knew her mother regarded it a special treat to visit Nannie and Aunt Sadie, who always had more than one kind of store bought cookie in their cupboard, and no one to fight over them. She was to stay with her relatives in Mattapan for a whole week.

But it's for a whole week. Still, what's the alternative? I could stay in this frigid old house and watch the icicles build on the eaves under the roof. Sit home and play cowboys and Indians, or house, or school with the peewees. The peewees were Glory's younger sisters and brother. *God, deadly.*

Glory reasoned with herself. *Really, I'll only miss Camille.*

Camille was Gloria's best friend. They met in French class the first day of high school, and had been the closest of friends ever since.

Camille is a real beauty, everybody says so.

Glory sometimes wondered why Camille wanted to be her friend.

She could be one of the popular crowd. She could have her pick of friends. I wonder why she likes me. Glory didn't think she deserved a friend as exquisite as Camille.

Back to Boston, Nannie lived around the corner from Franklin Park Zoo. Glory loved the elephant house, but it would be closed this time of year. She was starting to see a long, long week ahead of her.

I'll spend one good day in town, window shopping with Aunt Sadie. We'll buy hot peanuts from the street vendor, and maybe, even though it's winter, an ice cream sundae at Bailey's. We'll buy Jordan Marsh blueberry muffins to bring home for breakfast, and have one nice dainty proper lunch in town. Probably stop in at Fannie Farmer's for ribbon candy and Jordan almonds to bring home to Ma, then take the subway and the bus back. That day will most likely be Tuesday, if the weather holds.

But Wednesday…Thursday…Friday…Saturday. Glory dreaded the thought. *I'll be watching Aunt Sadie play solitaire for a solid week, and have to listen to Nannie complain about how the neighborhood is going downhill. And it's not like they'll let me go anywhere on my own. They'll think it's too dangerous, that maybe I'll end up in the bad part of town where the street walkers and muggers live.*

Gloria had hitched into Boston on more than one occasion, and taken the bus it seemed like a hundred times. *I can take care of myself. But of course, I can't tell them that. I'll have to play the sweet little princess. Bored out of my goddamn gourd.*

"Ma, do you think I could invite Camille to go with me?" Glory asked hopefully.

"Glory, you know they don't have enough for Camille. Besides, they want to see you, not your friend." Joyce couldn't keep the annoyance with her daughter out of her voice. "Maybe you'll go to a Saturday matinee. Look in the paper and see what movies are playing." Nothing's ever good enough, Joyce thought. I'd have killed for ice cream and shopping downtown when I was her age. Only fifteen and already bored with the world. She shook her head. Kids today. They don't know how good they have it.

~~~~~~

The next morning was Monday, the day that Glory would drive in with Dad to the city. Dad worked at the machine works in Quincy. That was close enough to Mattapan for him to give her a ride on his way to work, as long as they left early.

Herb normally got up at five thirty. He woke to a hacking cough that sounded like he could keel over and die any minute. This was the result of smoking cigarettes from age fourteen. Herb would sit on the edge of his bed, hack and cough and hack some more. Then he'd light up a Pall Mall, get dressed, and wash up.

He'd step outside to start up the car and clear off the windshield. He let the car run a good five or ten minutes every day before leaving. It was Herb's theory that warming up the car helped it to last longer. It was worth the price of the extra gas. He'd had a run of good luck with the last three old black Buicks. Herb applied the same logic to himself. He would have a shot of whiskey to get his blood flowing, and be out the door by six.

Monday through Friday, it would be the same every day. Herb stopped at the same doughnut shop along the way. He'd arrive by six thirty. He'd sit at the counter, order a plain doughnut and a jelly filled, smoke another Pall Mall, and nurse two cups of black coffee before heading off again around seven.

He enjoyed the talk he heard around him at the counter. A quiet man, Herb almost never said anything, but considered himself part of the conversation anyway.

There'd be men just like him, hard working men out early to make a living for their families - some young kids, some World War Two and Korean war vets, some phonies who never saw a day of action but liked to think they had. Herb had no tolerance for those guys with big opinions but nothing to back it up. If they actually served in the war, he thought, they'd be trying to forget it, not crow about it.

Today, they woke at five, to be out the door by five thirty.

A supreme sacrifice, like waking from the dead. Hades himself would understand. Up before dawn – the pits.

She'd had to pack her bag the night before. Dad hadn't been upstairs in more than five years, since a squirrel got into the attic and had to be taken care of. He wasn't about to start now just because Glory might be too lazy to get herself out of bed. And he wasn't about to leave late, not even one minute late.

From her upstairs bedroom, Glory heard her father's terrible coughing. She listened for a long time while he struggled to catch his breath and get up out of bed.

She dressed and tried to brush her hair. *Christ, as usual all tangled.* Glory tied it back with a ribbon. *I'll have all day at Nannie's to get the knots out. Nothing else to do anyway.* She picked up her suitcase and walked down the stairs. Dad was taking his shot of whiskey. Then out the door they went.

She was asleep in the car when they stopped for their breakfast. It was a half hour earlier than usual; Herb's regular crowd wasn't there yet. He'd been looking forward to showing off his beautiful daughter to his early morning friends. Herb was proud of Gloria from at least that one point of view.

Yet he found her immensely irritating most of the time and tried to stay away. He didn't know why; there was just something about her that kept him anxious and on guard; unhappy to be alone with her. He avoided time together with her, but wasn't sure what that was all about. Because he liked spending time with Penny, his older daughter, and of course the little ones, Kit and Suzi. It was only Gloria, his beauty, he had a hard time being with.

The customers in the doughnut shop tensed up when Herb and Glory walked in. They sat on stools at the counter and ordered. She got an expensive orange juice. Herb checked his pockets and ordered only one jelly doughnut and coffee.

"Hey, who's the broad? Here, girlie, girlie," a man on the other side of the counter teased. "Ooh baby, come to Papa!" his friend added. They laughed, obviously pleased with their crude banter.

Glory stared at the counter and shook her head. *What freaks.* She sipped her juice. It was fresh squeezed and had bits of pulp suspended in it. *I hate real orange juice. Should have gotten hot chocolate.*

"I'd like myself some of that there woman," the first man continued. He was an ugly man with a bulbous nose. *Looks like a drunk.*

She forced herself to drink the juice. *There are idiots and savages all around. And no one to defend me from them. It was no wonder Queen Elizabeth sent scouts to the new world while she herself stayed home. It's boring being safe, but probably, better than being abused. I thought idiot jerks were only in my backwater town, but in fact, they're everywhere.*

Someday, I'll be free to go wherever I want, whenever I want. It will be a new world, and no dumb creeps will stop me from getting there. She took some small comfort in her thoughts.

"Knock it off, will you? This is my daughter here." Herb said angrily. "Show some respect."

The men didn't care about Glory's feelings. They were men's men, with no real respect for any woman. But they mumbled their apologies to Herb. They knew you couldn't tease a man about his daughter, or his wife, his sister or mother. They were beyond comment. You had to save your remarks for the whores and broads of the world, and there were plenty of those all around.

Herb told Glory just to ignore them. "There are stupid people everywhere," he said.

They drove through the lower mills, past Baker's chocolate factory with its sweet cocoa aroma permeating the air, proclaiming its perfumed presence for all the world to acknowledge, and into Mattapan. Herb dropped Glory off at his mother-in-law's apartment on Columbia Road right at seven. That gave him just enough time to back track to Quincy and clock in at seven thirty.

Herb felt a great measure of relief — he had been alone with his daughter and the trip hadn't been so bad. When it was time to pick her up again, the following Sunday, the whole family would drive in for a visit. He was off the hook, at least until the next February school vacation.

~~~~~

Glory rang the bell at her grandmother's apartment. They buzzed her in. She walked up the three flights of stairs to the door they'd left open for her. Aunt Sadie was in the living room, finishing up her game of solitaire. She glanced up at Glory.

She's thinking, when was the last time I brushed my hair?

Nannie, always prompt and planning ahead, was preparing a nice potato and salmon salad for their lunch. She greeted Gloria with a happy smile. "Honey, your hair's a mess," she said. "Let Aunt Sadie help you with the tangles. But first, would you be a dear and get me the light rye out of the bread box? I meant to make a challah, but rye will have to do."

Glory did as she was told. She checked the sparkling clean bread box and found the light rye. She saw a tin of sugar cookies and a small box of chocolate biscuits.

Both waiting for someone to pay attention and notice they are there.

It was against her nature to be patient.

I'm trying though – give me credit. I want to stuff those cookies right into my mouth, to lay claim on them before anyone else.

But she remembered, reminded herself.

Even a queen has to wait, sometimes for years, for news from across the sea. Savages are everywhere. And the new world I'm longing for is oceans away.

THE MAPLES

Kit was ecstatic with Glory away at Nannie's for a week. There was no one to tell her to mind her own business, no one to rudely insist she vacate their one working bathroom. No one to tease her about her bangs that were in her eyes and needed cutting. No one to treat her like she was a mere pawn on a chess board, up against a mighty queen.

So when Glory returned from vacation, Kit took to sulking. "Ma," she moaned, "why doesn't Glory go back to Boston and live with Nannie? It would be so much better without her. I could take her bed and then I wouldn't have to share with Suzi." Kit envisioned a Gloria-free utopia where no one told her what to do.

Joyce looked up from her *New York Times* crossword puzzle. She thought of the poor McDonald family, a few houses down the street, whose oldest boy had just come home in a coffin. Friendly fire, so they said. Joyce despised the Vietnam war with her whole being. No matter what Herb said. He was a World War Two vet, a different case altogether. Something worth fighting for. This so-called conflict in Vietnam was another story. It sapped the strength of our nation and gave nothing in return. In Joyce's less than humble opinion.

"Don't be absurd, Kit. Can you check and see if the milkman came today? I think he missed our delivery." Ma paused. She knew her next sentence would bring groans of misery. "Oh, I might have to send you over to Stetson's farm for a couple of bottles of fresh-from-the-cow milk. Mmmm, with the cream floating on the top." Joyce's eyes sparkled in the teasing of Kit, who could be all too serious at times.

"Yuck! That's disgusting! With those little globs of blobby cream in my glass? Gross!" Kit was horrified. She was young enough not to have experienced much of the days of unhomogenized milk. Homogenization was a modern convenience and the salvation of children everywhere who didn't like milk in any form except chocolate.

"Get your coat and hat on. And find Glory. She can go with you." Joyce could be deliciously cruel, but she ended her taunt there. "And while you're at the farm," she said in a conciliatory manner, "see if they've got any fresh maple syrup boiled up yet. I think sugaring season started last week."

Kit perked up with talk of maple syrup. Mr. Stetson was known for giving out free samples of maple sugar candy. It hurt her teeth to bite into the concoction, being so sweet, but the small amount of pain was worth it for the uniquely delicate treat.

She yelled up the stairs. "Glory, Ma says we have to go to Stetson's! I'm leaving now. You can catch up." Kit threw on her winter coat and stuffed her hat into her pocket. It was an unseasonably warm late February day, and she was no baby. She didn't need to be told to wear a hat. She grabbed the three dollars Ma dug out of her pocketbook and skipped out the door.

~~~~~~

Joyce returned to her crossword. 14 Across. Hmm, she thought, what's a four letter word for casket? Oh, that's easy – cist. This is easy, too easy. 10 Down. An eleven letter word for war? Oh for God's sake – hostilities. What do they think I am, a beginner?

~~~~~

February can be the coldest and snowiest month of the year in southeastern Massachusetts. But this particular February was milder than anyone remembered going years back. Farmers took advantage of the fresh air and sunshine to put their animals out to pasture, even though the grass was brown and shriveled into hard stone-like patches. Mothers did the same, sending their kids out to play. It was a rare delight for the season.

The deciduous trees were all bare of course, their brown branches like interlocking lace against a flawless sapphire sky. For no matter how powerful, Mother Nature cannot move the young buds along to unfold any sooner than is their due. In this regard only, humans with their instincts and abilities to adapt have an edge over the rotating but fixed track of the seasonal earth.

The warming days and cool nights of February and March create the push and pull that draws the sap of maples from their roots up to the top branches. The coursing sap is the sugar, the life blood of the maple tree, preparing itself for a spring explosion of thousands of hand sized leaves and helicopter shaped seeds that children everywhere stick on their noses in delight.

Industrious Yankees and native peoples have tapped the sugar maples for centuries, every year at the same time, draining out buckets of the sap and boiling it down in sugar houses to make maple syrup. One gallon of maple syrup requires forty gallons of maple sap boiled down and strained. The result is literal nectar of the forest gods, a syrup with a sweet earthiness. A flavor of both hidden root and swaying branch, of gaining light and frosty eves, of crusty snow and melting droplets, incomparable to other tastes.

~~~~~~

Kit cut through the new side street that had recently been paved down the road. She passed the stand of Concord grape vines, withered and brown now with ice-covered un-plucked fruit but the promise of late summer ahead, and turned the corner at the giant hemlock toward Stetson's dairy farm. She skipped along the pathway that led a half mile later to the farmstead. The route was lined with barbed wire fence on either side.

"Mares eat oats and does eat oats, and little lambs eat ivy, a kid will eat ivy too, wouldn't you?" sang Kit with a relish. Faster, she challenged herself. "Maresy dotes and doesey dotes and little lamsy divey a kiddledee divey too wouldn't you? Faster! Maresy dotesand doeseydotes andlittlelamsydivey akiddledeediveytoo wouldn'tyou?" She tried to sing it three times on one breath. She was free, on her own, and didn't need anyone to tell her what to do.

In a bit she slowed down and sniffed the sunny cool air. Ugh, cow poop, disgusting! That smell! It's getting stronger by the second, thought the little girl with the need for a haircut and independence.

~~~~~~

"She loves you…" Glory shouted out to the lacey maples as she rounded the bend by the hemlock. *Paul. Oh my God, he is SO dreamy.*

Of all the Beatles, Paul is far and away the most handsome. Best singer. Most unbelievable dreamboat of the group. Who could argue with that? Can't think of a single friend who would disagree. Even Penny can't argue that Paul is the cutest. Though she thinks John has the most talent. And George is cute, really cute. Ringo, well Ringo is a great drummer, enough said. But it's okay because Paul makes up for everything. Paul.

As she strolled down the path, Glory turned her face to Apollo, the youthful sun god.

Paul.

She tilted her chin to absorb the rare February light.

Paul, my love.

She closed her eyes to feel Apollo's strength.

Paul, my…

And down she went, tripping on a frozen tree root sticking out of the hard rock road. "Ouch!" Glory cried in indignation. She had never been handled so rudely by a god before. Mother Nature, surely, all the time. Goddesses, yes. But gods had a rather special place for Glory in their hearts. She wasn't used to such treatment. Her dignity shattered for the moment.

But the queen in her recovered quickly. She stood up, pushed back her curly tangled hair off her face and brushed her bottom off, and started down the road again. She rounded another bend, and stopped with surprise.

Oh, God, this is so embarrassing!

There was Kit, screeching and climbing frantically into the branches of a big old maple tree beyond. And three brown bony cows stood nosing each other at the base of the tree.

Kit yelled out. "Glory, help me!" She had the panicked look of a swimmer surrounded by sharks. She flailed her arms at the cows, shooing them away from above.

"Hahahahahahaha!" Glory shrieked. "What in the world are you doing?"

Kit scrambled higher in the branches. She caught her sneaker on a metal spike sticking out of the tree, and knocked down one of Farmer Stetson's syrup taps and bucket, getting sticky sap on her jacket as she hugged the tree trunk. She looked down at the cows, who were now mooing their discontent with Kit.

"Help!" cried Kit. "They're gonna get me!" Just then a wasp, which had been unseasonably awakened on this February day, flew past Kit's nose. "Ahhhhhhhhhh!" she screamed.

Glory fell onto the rocky road in hysterical glee. "Moo! Moo!" she sputtered, helpless with painful laughter. "Moooooooooooo!!"

The cows moved to the dropped bucket, looking for feed. They tipped it over. The maple sap spilled onto the ground. They crowded round, lapping up the watery substance, forgetting Kit for the time being.

Glory tried not to moo. She tried not to wheeze. The annoying task of accompanying baby sister Kit for milk with cream on the top had transformed into entertainment of a lifetime.

Kit sniffled and hiccoughed. "The fence...is...broken over there...and the cows came through, and they...started to chase me, and...I almost stepped into poop, and then they...they started to run at me, and then...then." Kit broke into tears. "Then I climbed the tree so they wouldn't bite me."

"Hahahahahahahahahahahahahaha!" roared Glory. She fell down again and rolled on the ground. "Ow, ow, my sides hurt!"

It took some small time for her to regain a measure of control as Kit continued to bawl and hiccough. "You idiot, Kit, the cows aren't going to bite you!"

"Yes...they are," Kit hiccoughed defensively.

"No, they're not." Glory was sure. "These are tired old cows, all they want is grass. They don't want to eat you."

Christ, even city girls know that cows can be bossy but they aren't out to get you.

"She's right, you know." From across the field, Farmer Stetson had heard the yelling and took in the scene. "This one here, she's old Betsy, the oldest cow I got. And that one, she's Buttercup. Gives the creamiest milk. And the other, that's Mabel, she's a sweet old thing. Not one of them will bite you, miss.

But what do I see here? What's this hubbub? You've gone and

knocked down a whole bucket of my sap? Well, that's a shame. Did you know it takes forty of them buckets to make one of maple syrup? Yep, 40 to 1. That bucket'll cost me."

"We're sorry, Mr. Stetson," Glory explained. "Kit got scared. She didn't know better. Come on down, Kit."

Glory reached her arms out to Kit, whose face was streaked with tears and jacket covered in sap. But it was the farmer who helped her down out of the tree. Kit glared furiously at Glory.

"Ain't you that Jewish family down the way? I heard there was a tribe of them down near the field."

"Yes, we're Jewish." Glory tried not to bristle. *What difference does it make what we are?* "And we've got three dollars, so we can pay you for the sap."

Together they walked to the barn where Farmer Stetson had just finished milking half his herd. "Would you like to taste some milk right from the cow?" he asked sincerely. "There's nothin' better in this world, I guarantee."

Bacchus, save me. I've never tasted wine except that once at Passover at Auntie Miriam's when they finally figured out I'm past the age for grape juice. God, it was horrible. Disgusting. I practically hurled it. But even that was better than this milk will be. Ugh - straight from the cow.

Both Glory and Kit despised milk unless it was doused with chocolate syrup, and doubted his word. But they were raised to be polite, and soon enough, they were tasting small cups of milk direct from the udder.

I'm going to gag.

The girls had always drunk refrigerated milk. They hadn't anticipated that fresh milk would be warm, almost hot to match the cow's insides. It was like Nannie's hot milk before bed cure for insomnia. Everyone's nightmare.

Kit couldn't help herself. She ran through the barn and retched out the milk just past the door.

Swallow. You are a queen, act like one.

"Thanks very much, Mr. Stetson," Glory managed to utter. "That was different. I've never had anything like that before. I almost forgot, we'll need two bottles of milk for the road, please."

I almost forgot because I'm going to upchuck right here on the barn floor.

"Aren't you going to buy some of my maple syrup?" Farmer Stetson asked. "That's fresh too, just boiled it down yesterday."

"Well, we don't have enough money now that Kit spilled the sap."

"Oh, don't worry about that, little lady, I was just jokin' you. I get on my high horse over nothin' sometimes. Here, take a quart with you. And don't forget to bring all them bottles back for refills next time you come."

Glory and Kit started back down the road toward home, holding their pained and bruised stomachs all the way. They were disappointed not to have been offered any maple sugar candy, as gossip had suggested they would. But still, they got their milk and maple syrup, and wouldn't have to explain anything at all to Ma. It was a fair trade that they resolved to keep to themselves. Even though Kit wasn't about to forgive Glory for laughing at her. And for leaving her at the mercy of those mean old cows.

Farmer Stetson watched them leave. "Those girls are mighty pretty," he said to timeworn Betsy, who was now in the pen ready to be milked next. "Surprisin' they're Jews. I thought all Jews had big noses. And Jews are damn cheap, so I've heard. Nothin' cheap about those two. Hmm, but Jews don't believe in Jesus, so I've heard. I'd be interested in seeing what the whole tribe looks like. Confusin', damn confusin'." He adjusted his glasses and watched the two girls disappear around the bend by his tallest hemlock. Then he turned and readied old Betsy for the business of the day.

~~~~~

Joyce rolled up the *Times* crossword puzzle and with it, smacked a house fly that had the misfortune to wake prematurely in late February in the mess under her kitchen table. She left it where it perished on the floor, settled back into her chair, and took a drag on her Chesterfield. 12 Down. Seven letter word for flag. Pennant, that's easy. 6 Across. Battle, five letter word. Okay, now it's getting tougher. Oh yes, melee. 7 Down. Nine letter word for massacre. Damn war. There's no escaping it.

MARCH

It was late March in a rural corner of southeastern Massachusetts, and that could mean only one thing – mud. Mud, and lots of it. Mud in the street, mud covering the sidewalk, mud in the field. Every goddamn thing I see is covered in mud, thought Joyce. Joyce was a city girl who hadn't experienced the seasons, really, until she moved with Herb and the kids out to the country.

First, they'd settled only ten miles or so out from Boston, in the next town out from Herb's sister, Miriam. They lived in a small white house with giant pine trees, trees so big and so broad that Penny and Glory had mapped out a pretend house underneath with pine needle rooms and plenty of space to play. The young sisters lay down picnic cloths and served imaginary tea and cookies to their favorite dolls and stuffed bears. They played house for hours on end. Sometimes other girls in the neighborhood joined them, but mostly they played by themselves. They were best friends, alone and together.

Often Duke joined them under the trees. Duke was a mutt that Herb found begging for food at the back door. He had fed the dog a few scraps, and Duke became part of their family.

Duke followed Glory around. He liked her best. When she was very little and they first moved to the house, Joyce put her outside in a carriage for a nap. Duke guarded Glory. He wouldn't let anyone near her. He'd growl even at Joyce. Joyce had asked Herb to get rid of that mangy mutt, but Herb refused. He thought it was kind of funny, just a little, that Duke made his presence known.

Under the trees was a girls place only – no boys allowed. The neighborhood boys had their own tree and built a rickety fort in it. The boys loved their fort though it was nothing more than a few planks nailed into the trunk. They usually left the girls alone. But still, Penny's twin brother Sammy rushed through the girls' pines from time to time to establish his domain. He didn't want anyone to forget who was king.

Unless it was really pouring, even in the snow and rain the girls and all their household goods stayed dry and protected under the pine branches. It wasn't the Hundred Acre Wood – perhaps Christopher Robin would have poo-pooed it. He was a boy and needed more space. But to Penny and Glory it was more than good enough; the trees were the girls' world.

Herb and Joyce, Sammy, Penny, and Glory had come all the way out there, past most family and familiar streets, past theaters and pubs, past the swan boats and public gardens, past all they had known because rents were lower for a house big enough to hold them all. Even so, they might have been happy to stay. But Joyce had a miscarriage when Glory was almost three. She fell into a sadness she hadn't experienced in many years. Then Kit came along, and Suzi. Their family grew too big for the small white house with the giant pine trees you couldn't climb because you'd get too sappy, but you could pretend to be queens of the forest and be happy under for hours on end.

They moved farther out, much farther, to an old tumble down farmhouse in the middle of nowhere. It was an hour from anywhere.

In true Yankee fashion, the house was built in stages, with a formal parlor in the front and plainer rooms behind. As a second floor, a decommissioned one room schoolhouse was moved to the site when the Academy opened. A warren of upper rooms and two large attics completed the house.

The property was a potato farm. A hundred years before, the

Levasseur family suffered a major loss. After years of hard labor turning the rocky soil into a working farm, their only son died from tuberculosis. They had four girls, but no one to take on the running of the farm. It was dirty, messy work, routing in the mud, turning dirt with flat headed shovels so as not to bruise the tender new potatoes. It was work not fit for girls.

Madame Levasseur was more than naturally distressed by her son's death. She became moody and difficult; overly stern toward her daughters. At times it seemed she was going mad. "Mon petit, mon petit!" she would cry, searching the house day and night for her dead son.

Had they settled only several miles farther south, they might have farmed cranberries in the soft sandy soil that stretched all the way to the tip of Cape Cod. Or, they might have converted to a dairy and raised cows like some of their more foresighted neighbors. Figure out how to turn a living in the poor stone filled dirt.

But Monsieur Levasseur didn't know cows and didn't have the money to invest in a proper barn to house livestock. It was decided to sell off the farm and move back home to Quebec where people spoke their native language. It would be easier for Maman once back with her family – maybe she would heal. Madame Levasseur didn't go willingly. She had to be carried out of the house where she imagined the spirit of her son living on for all eternity.

When they sold the property, it was divided into lots and sold off one by one. The town purchased close to a hundred acres directly across the unpaved road from the farmhouse, and later built a school and playing fields. Eventually most of the fields gave way to housing. All around the original farmhouse, smaller houses were built on little side streets cut into the meadows. The road was paved, then widened. Soon enough, you couldn't tell an old potato farm had ever existed.

One hundred years after the Levasseur's moved out, Glory's family moved in. The house was drafty and poorly maintained, but it had room for them all, with a maple tree in the back that you could climb on. Across the street was a field and beyond that, the middle school. The field had a playground with swings and two baseball diamonds, lacrosse fields, tennis courts, a football field with a track circling it, and expanses of green meadow, a brook, and woods. The field was every child's dream. It was the Hundred Acre Wood come true.

They hadn't lived there long when Duke, wanting to play with the kids in the field, ran into the street and was hit by a car. He had followed Glory and didn't look while crossing. To give Duke credit, he was out of his element; an old dog in a new place and a busy, busy road. It should have been expected. It was just a matter of time.

Davey was born and the family complete. They might have been happy. But no matter how hard she tried to appreciate her new home for the sake of their children, Joyce still hated it. Not the house, which, though never fancy had a certain comfort about it despite its many flaws, but the town. The land in the middle of nowhere. The endless monotony of the woods and the fields. The lack of companionship, of sophistication of any sort. The dearth of excitement, of city sounds and sights.

The worst, the part that Joyce couldn't get used to was the blatant relentlessness of her natural surroundings. A realization of how little control she had over her environment. She'd had no idea. She hadn't understood the true force or full fury or messy underside of Mother Nature.

Joyce remembered red brick buildings and gas lanterns; city pavement and cobblestone streets. Your way might have been frozen over or covered with snow or dirt, but you weren't up to your hips in mud, for Christ's sake. You could duck into a doorway if you got too cold. The trolleys ran no matter what the weather.

You could get where you had to go. Joyce didn't drive, like many women of her generation. Herb took their one car to work every day. She hadn't known what isolation could mean, what true loneliness was until she came to their small cow town, miles from everything she knew.

~~~~~

Penny shoved her feet into the old grey rubber boots by the back door. She threw on Dad's worn black coat and twisted a lumpy rust colored wool scarf around her neck. She had the unenviable task of bringing the kitchen garbage out to the garbage pail that was sunk into the ground by the drive. Penny wasn't happy about it. She mumbled all the way. "Why am I stuck with this disgusting job?" she said to herself. "Where's Sammy – he should be doing this."

She carried out the stinking garbage - table scraps, rotten fruit and leftovers, vegetable shavings and moldy bread - everything except for bones and meat scraps. All this was separated out for the pigs. Mr. Cormier had a contract with the town for his pig farm. He picked up the slop from the townspeople's tables and fed it to his animals, which would eat almost anything, even corn cobs. This kept down the amount of trash going to the dump. It was a good system and worked well.

Penny hoisted the bucket with three or four days-worth of food that was inedible by human standards. She waded through the muddy areas and slush puddles in the yard to the sunken garbage pail beyond. Her boots were covered in mud halfway up to her knees.

She got to the pail by the drive, and stepped down with her muddy boot on the lever that opened the pail lid. The lid sprang open. Penny poured her bucket of slop into the open pail and let her foot off the lever. The lid closed shut. There, she thought, I've done my awful duty.

A dog barked. Penny stepped back to see whose dog was coming up the drive. As she did, her boot slipped in the half frozen mud. She tumbled down onto the ice filled mud and rolled down a slight incline into a patch of evergreens still covered with snow. She landed against them with a thump, and a shower of snow fell down onto her.

Penny looked around with some delight even though she was covered in mud. She was a little stunned. Though she was big, seventeen, and the branches were small, it seemed she was back in her very own pine needle pretend home under the giant pines by the small white house. She rested against an evergreen trunk, feeling a little dizzy. Perhaps she had hit her head without knowing.

As she sat and tried to regain her balance, the barking collie from down the road came into the yard. "Here, Shep!" she called to him. Shep ran across the mud and sneaked under the pine branches. He gave Penny a big lick right in the face. She hugged him and thought of Duke, her trusty old friend.

~~~~~~

"Hurry up and choose, Glory," six year old Penny said excitedly to her little sister. "Do you want a Chunky or a candy necklace? Or maybe five different things?" Glory had a nickel to spend, and believe it or not, that would buy a whole candy bar or several pieces of penny candy.

Glory stood looking through the glass case. She couldn't make up her mind. The case was filled with candies and fudge and mysterious pastries. There were too many things to choose from. "C'mon Glory," said Penny. "We want to get back to our play house. I want to decorate the picnic area with my pretty purple ribbon."

Penny had purchased three penny candies and spent a whole dime on her satin ribbon. She was anxious to get back to play under the pines. Most of that winter had been much too cold to stay outside for long. March had come and it was still cold, but if you bundled up you could play for a while in the protected warmth of the trees. Today was their first day in the pines. But before they settled in, they walked down to the center of town to buy candy at The Golden Slipper. They would have a party to celebrate the coming of spring.

Madame Helena sat in the back of The Golden Slipper. She was draped in red, gold, and purple scarves like an old gypsy lady. She wore scarves over her black hair and many strings of beads around her neck.

It was hard for Penny to understand how such a woman could be here in their plain old town. Madame was nothing like anyone else Penny knew. Her store, The Golden Slipper, was a marvel of mystery. It was run down and a bit dirty, but Penny and Glory both believed they would never see anything more exotic and beautiful.

There were scarves and beads, tiny statues, and necklaces made of stones and feathers. Madame had stained glass panels that hung on little ribbons. There were balls of pure blown glass in brilliant colors hanging in the windows. She sold delicate laces and shiny satin ribbons, and brocade tapestries. And of course, most importantly, there was the glass case filled with candies of every description.

Madame was sitting by her wood stove playing solitaire. She stood up and smiled at the girls. "Mademoiselle Penelope," she nodded warmly to Penny as she handed her the bag with Penny's candy and ribbon. She had seen the girls many times before and knew them well, as she did most of the children in town. "Ma petit Gloria," she whispered fondly. "Having a hard time choosing today? Let me look into my crystal ball. Perhaps it will give you a hint."

Staring intently at an amethyst globe hanging in the window, "hmm..." Madame said, "the lucky stars are telling me something. What could it be? Ah yes, it becomes clearer. They are saying, a girl like you, who cares for beauty even at this tender age, deserves a special treat. A lovely candy necklace, to delight your eyes as well as your tummy. What do you think, little one? A candy necklace?"

Glory stared in amazement at Madame Helena. *How does Madame know the candy necklace is exactly what I want?* Penny was dumbfounded too. It was a beautiful mystery. Gloria paid her nickel. Madame wrapped her candy in a small white paper bag. They said their goodbyes, and the two sisters headed home in the cold March air.

They had a good long walk ahead of them, three quarters of a mile or more. Just outside the store, Glory stopped.

Must take off my mittens. They're ugly orange and there's a hole in the thumb. They're not beautiful. She took off her mittens, stuffed them into her pockets, and continued on, holding her little bag tightly in her bare hands.

As they walked, the wind picked up. You couldn't trust March weather. One minute there'd be a strong sun shining and mud everywhere. The next, snow or a howling bitter wind and everything would freeze. You just never knew.

They walked along in the chilly cold for quite some time. They still had a quarter mile to go when Penny said, "Come on Glory, let's run." She couldn't wait to get back under the pines where it would be warmer and not so windy. She started to jog down the road, leaving her four year old sister behind. To give Penny credit, she was only six herself. Penny thought, Glory will catch up soon enough. She kept going and didn't look back.

But Glory couldn't run. She could barely walk. Her bare hands were frozen.

I'm so cold. My hands hurt. They're all red. She wouldn't let go of her candy bag to put her hands inside her pockets or put on her mittens. Truthfully, she was a small child and probably didn't think to do so. She struggled her way down the street, and then it started to snow.

Penny raced to the pine trees at the edge of her yard. She beat the snow by seconds. Her face was red and freezing. She laughed at the cold. She was in her protected pine needle house, and all was well. She thought about where to hang her beautiful satin ribbon. She took a root beer barrel out of her bag and sucked on it. "Mmmm, it's good, isn't it, Duke?" she commented to her best dog friend. Duke had been taking a nap in the pine needles. When Penny arrived, he stood up, shook himself off, and greeted her with a lick on the face.

The snow fell a little harder. Glory's hands couldn't move. They were frozen to the bag.

My legs are sore. I don't want to walk anymore. My eyes are tired. She leaned against a telephone pole and decided to rest.

Just then, a man in a felt hat and top coat walked by. He stopped and looked at Gloria. Glory wasn't a crier. Even at age four, no one could remember the last time she'd cried. But she couldn't stop herself now. The tears ran down her cheeks and felt warm against her skin.

I'm cold, so cold. And where is Penny? He said, "Little girl, where do you live? I'll take you home." Glory pointed down the street. *Not supposed to talk to strangers.*

The man picked her up and carried her down the street. Glory closed her eyes. *So tired and cold. Need to rest.* The man didn't ask if they were close to home. He held her tightly and kept walking.

Penny finished her root beer barrel. She hung her ribbon on the branch above the teddy bears' picnic spot. She began to wonder what was taking Glory so long to come home when Duke started a long, low growl. "Duke, stop it." Penny said. "Don't be mean to Teddy." Penny thought Duke was jealous, just a little, of Penny's best bear friend.

Duke let out another growl, and then started to bark. He barked up a winter storm of barks. Then he barreled out from underneath the pines and dashed to the street. Penny wondered what Duke had to bark about. Where was he going in all that snow? she wondered.

There was something in Duke's bark that sounded bad. Like he knew something was wrong, really wrong. Penny ran out from under the protection of her pine tree. She followed Duke's barking noise. She got out to the street and saw Duke. He was growling and snapping at a man in a long coat. The man was carrying Glory down the street.

Penny didn't stop to think. She raced into her house. "Mama! Mama!" she called. "Come quick!" Joyce was having a cup of coffee and reading a magazine in the living room. She had heard Duke bark, and was just about to look out the window to see what the fuss was all about. She glanced out, and ran in her slippers out the front door.

Duke had planted his bared teeth on the man's pant leg when Ma arrived. "Down, Duke, down," she commanded. Duke stopped but sat on his haunches growling his long, low growl. Ma confronted the man. She said, "This is my daughter. Please give her to me." Ma was shivering from the cold but determined. She held out her arms to the man.

The man stood thinking. He paused as though considering his next step, and said, "Sorry, ma'am. I didn't mean no harm. The little girl fell asleep, and I didn't know where to drop her off." The man gave Gloria back to Ma.

"Thank you," she said. "Good day." She turned and carried

Glory into the house while the man walked away. She locked the door behind her, something she never thought to do.

Joyce wasn't sure what to believe. Was the man good? She didn't know. But she thanked her lucky stars that Duke loved Glory best and would guard her against all threats, real or imagined. That night, for the first time ever Ma fed Duke right off the table. She gave him an entire frankfurter, bun and all.

When they got inside, Penny helped Ma warm up her little sister. They wrapped her in a big fuzzy blanket. They held her frozen hands in theirs, and brought a tub of warm water to keep the stinging sensation away. They made hot chocolate and ate gingerbread with whipped cream.

Penny liked to be a help to Ma. She felt grown up and like a mother herself. Joyce thought, whatever would I do without my level headed Penny?

When Glory felt back to normal, she put on her candy necklace. She admired herself in the mirror. "Don't you just love my pretty necklace?" she asked Ma. Joyce smiled and said "Yes, it's beautiful. But there is also beauty in a pair of old orange mittens with a hole in the thumb. Someday when you're older, I think you'll understand."

~~~~~~

Penny stood up. She shook the snow off her hat and coat. She petted Shep and told him to go home. She picked up the empty garbage bucket and threaded her way back across the yard, through the mud and slush puddles to the back door. She left the muddy boots and Dad's old coat just inside.

Ma was in the kitchen smoking a Chesterfield. "Hey Ma," Penny said, "do you remember the old house and the giant pines? Remember how Glory and I used to play underneath for hours and hours? Even in the snow and the mud?"

Joyce nodded. She remembered that time when everyone seemed happier. When even she felt more content with herself and her place in the world. When Miriam was well and full of life.

Of course it wasn't a perfect time. There was the miscarriage. And the weather. There was mud and wind and ice storms and rain. The month of March was much the same. There's not much you can do about the weather in March. If you don't like it, wait a minute – it will change.

SAMMY

Sammy was acting impossible again, for the umpteenth time that day. *He always thinks he's so great,* thought Glory. He had just come back from the track meet in the field across the street. He was all sweaty and gross and full of energy. "Guess what?" he said. "I won first place in the 100 meter dash, and second in the relay!" Sammy's room was filled with blue, red, and yellow ribbons and several trophies too.

"That's nice," Glory said without conviction. *Who cares about stupid sports.*

To keep in shape, she and her best friend Camille had the habit of running the track that circled the football field. They were up to four times around, about a mile, and as a result had each lost a little off their waistlines. Jogging was fun until the boys found them, which somehow they always did, crowding around making rude comments. *Pimply-faced savages. We don't need an audience of gawking commoners.* They would laugh and made filthy gestures.

Camille hated it. She turned borscht red every time. *That's a laugh in itself,* Glory had to admit. She wasn't so prim and first thought the attention was fun. She knew she was, as they said, built like a brick shithouse. After a while she realized that *one, I can't help how I'm built; and two, they are disgusting pigs.*

She complained to Ma, who said, "Boys will be boys."

Face it, even the greatest queen of all, Elizabeth, probably endured crude and boorish men who were only after one thing. No wonder she never married. Glory and Camille learned to stick to tennis, which didn't seem to interest the boys as much. *Maybe because it's the ball that's bouncing, not me.*

~~~~~

Sammy danced around the living room in victory. He twisted the damp towel that hung around his neck, and whipped it at Glory. "Who's the greatest?" he demanded. Gloria wouldn't give him the satisfaction of a response. He snapped his towel at her again. She laughed at him as she ducked out of the way. She secretly delighted in the rough play that was meant to be only between boys. *Though of course I'm not about to let my smart aleck brother know it.*

As she turned, Sammy caught Glory's long dark braid that hung down her back. He gave a fierce pull that brought tears to Gloria's eyes. She tried to be stoic, to keep from crying. *Christopher.* In first grade, from his desk behind her, the bully had mercilessly tugged at her braid all year long. *I hated Christopher.* But Ma had said, "That means he likes you."

Glory knew that her mother had introduced her to something important. *One of the great secrets of the world. For the rest of first grade, I'd pretend to be a noble and haughty queen, and exhibit pointed disdain every time Christopher came near. But knowing that he liked me, made me like him back, just a little.*

~~~~~

Sammy was now launching spit balls to get her attention. *He never runs out of ways to torture me.* "Don't you dare hit me with those disgusting things again!" Glory turned back to face her older brother with all the courage she could muster. Her deep violet eyes glared at him with a fury that took him aback. *I am Mary, Queen of Scots, and I won't go down without a good fight!*

A good fight...I remember the time in the field when I was thirteen. It was a Sunday near dusk, and one of those sticky, clammy days that makes your shirt stick to your back. I was watching a pickup baseball game. There was nothing else to do.

Glory lived right across the street from the baseball diamond. She would have liked to play, but she could only watch. Boys were allowed to play organized sports and girls weren't. *It wasn't fair, but there it was.* Instead of playing, she walked over on this sweltering day in her baby doll top, cutoff shorts and flip flops, and sat by herself in the hot steel bleachers.

The boys were always showing off when they saw Gloria. *Stealing bases and sliding into home plate when they could practically have walked it.* She admired them their confidence and physical strength; their great sense of freedom and entitlement. *How they acted in teams like packs of wolves with no one out of step, all hungry for the same win.*

The game was a close one, three to two. The boys played extra hard in the heat of the day. After the game, it was almost dark. The players shook hands like good sports, and packed up to leave.

Gloria peeled her legs off the sweltering steel seat, swung over, and jumped off the side of the bleacher. She pulled at her clinging shirt. She wiped the dust that had blown up onto her shorts and thighs, and bent over to pick up the sandals that had fallen off when she jumped.

She stood up barefoot and faced a pack of boys, all looking at her. *As if they shared a single thought.* Even the young ones, middle school-ers, stared at her. They moved toward her with a single wordless spirit, their eyes squinting and tongues panting. Gloria took a sharp breath in. *What's happening?*

She stepped back and stung her bare arm on the hot bleacher. *The boys kept coming. Their shirts dripped with perspiration, their pants tightening.*

Gloria looked down. *My top, it's transparent, sweat soaked.* She thought hard. *Stand up straight and tall. Leave now, right away.*

She tossed her long curly hair in defiance, and started for the gate. *The stone driveway hurts, bites through the bottoms of my naked feet. Stand up straight, don't slouch. Show all the confidence I can muster, keep walking to the gate.*

Keep walking as though I am Mary, queen of all Scotland and maybe England too, if I play my cards right. I just need to keep my head. Stay calm. Now is not the time to panic. Just get through the gate. Back to home base.

There was something majestic in Gloria. After all, she seemed too big a meal for the pack. She was a prey too unattainable. Confused, the boys stepped aside and allowed her to pass. She thought, even then in her fright, *they're afraid – that's why they hate me. They don't understand what this hunger is inside them.*

As she neared the gate, she felt the first stone hit. *And then another, and another.* She glimpsed back and saw a solid wall of boys, each with the same strange wild appetite drawn sharply on his face. The pelting continued with a silent, frustrated frenzy. Glory shielded her head. *Run. Get through that gate.*

She ran past the iron rails and across the street into her yard, fighting back her tears. *No one should see a queen cry.* She got in the house and locked herself in the bathroom. Looking long and hard in the mirror, she felt repulsed by what she saw. *So this is sex,* she thought.

Gloria took a long bath and went to bed early. She didn't tell Ma what had happened. She knew she had learned another of life's great secrets, and didn't need her mother to explain it to her further.

~~~~~

Sammy grabbed Glory's arm and gave it a double twist. It made a sharp, searing pain from her elbow to her wrist. Gloria shrieked,

"Stop it, you jerk!" She punched at him, but Sammy was quick. He caught her hand, forced her fingers open, and stretched them apart until Glory cried, "uncle! uncle!"

Sammy laughed with the taste of victory. "Do you surrender then?" Glory was silent. "Do you surrender?" he insisted.

She refused to give in. "Who's the greatest?" Sammy crowed.

I have to admit that my brother is strong and quick, and, yes, he's smart.

"You are," she finally replied, knowing it was the truth. She kept the greater truth to herself.

DAVEY

Glory hurried down the street toward home. She had stayed late at school for another detention, far from the first time this year. Glory was an excellent student, near the top of her class. And invariably well behaved in school.

Ma insists on good manners. Why isn't being smart good enough for my teachers? I could scream, I'm so bored! But I do the work, don't I? Am I not always prepared?

At home, it was assumed that she do well in school. There was no prize. Glory knew some kids who got a dollar bill for every A. But no, not in this house. Not even a "job well done" or "good work, my dear!" It was simply expected. *The price one has to pay for living in this family with their impossible expectations.*

The teachers were always catching Glory in a day dream or staring out the classroom window. Mrs. Hansen, her history teacher, seemed to make a game of writing up detention slips. *I suppose it makes my sadistic, twisted, inhuman teacher happy.* Today, Mrs. Hansen was drilling the class on the succession of English monarchs.

Even though everyone knows that memorizing lists of long dead kings is an exercise that could make even the best student want to vomit. Worse even than studying the names and dates of battles and wars. Well, maybe it's a tie between the two for deadliest.

Gloria took a deep sigh and watched a daddy long legs on the ceiling. *Wonder if it's male or female.* Everyone she knew referred to all bugs as male, as though even in the bug world there were no females worth mentioning.

She had read a book on the life of Henry the Eighth last summer at the beach. *Fat pig who beheaded all his wives.* He had married the beautiful Spanish princess Catherine of Aragon. Then he divorced her when she couldn't give him a male heir to the English throne. She'd born a strong and lively daughter, Mary. *But no, apparently not good enough. Why wasn't a girl good enough for the king?*

The spider crawled along the ceiling tile toward the open window panel. *It's creeping upside down. I wonder how they do that?* Though she preferred tales of King Arthur and Robin Hood, Glory thought maybe her next book would be about spiders. *I'll be twenty five and still pretending Maid Marion. Maybe it's time to get real.*

Glory had read that the Pope had refused to grant the divorce, so King Henry disavowed the Catholic Church to marry again. He created his own church in protest, thrown his queen in the Tower, and taken his lover to wife. *To prison for life! Off with their heads! Some of the bloodiest history of all time in the making, all to get a son.*

This second wife, Anne Boleyn, also gave birth. *To a measly girl, Elizabeth. Who would become only the greatest queen of all time. But still, no prince for Henry to love. No boy child to give all his pride and all his fortunes to. Well, Mary and Elizabeth would just have to duke it out between themselves, and grab what they could along the way. Nothing new there.*

"Miss M____, are you still with us?" sneered Mrs. Hansen. "Can you tell me which monarch, which king was next in succession?" *A trick question for sure.*

Glory looked squarely at the teacher with her piercing violet eyes and replied in her straightforward way, as though she had been listening all along. "The great queen, Elizabeth the First, of course." The class burst out laughing - Glory was so good at showing up the teacher. Mrs. Hansen turned red, furiously scribbled out a pink detention note, and slapped it on Gloria's desk.

Glory looked up and saw the daddy long legs gone, escaped from the classroom. *The spider at least, is free.* She hoped with all the fierceness of her spirit that it was female.

~~~~~~

Crap, it's almost five, she worried as she raced home. Ma didn't make many rules. She had too many kids to enforce them anyway, and no inclination to restrain her children from experiencing the world.

Ma was what you might call a free thinker. One of the few things you could get into trouble over was not being home by five. *You could be dancing in Cambridge Common with the Hare Krishnas or thumbing your way home from Horseneck Beach for all she knew, but if you weren't home by five, you were in for a piece of her mind.*

Not that Gloria ever remembered being spanked – Ma didn't believe in such things. *But you could be restricted for a week if you were late for supper. Or two weeks, or even a month if you were caught smoking, or if she heard you swear. Being restricted, it goes without saying, is the pits. You have no friends, can't talk on the phone. You have to come home directly after school and can't go out on the weekends, not even to the field to watch a game or play tennis. Being restricted is to be avoided at all costs.*

Glory didn't need a key. Her house, like most in her small town, was never locked. It was a trusting time. She flew in the door with two minutes to spare, and was about to announce her triumphant return. She saw no one home. *Where is everybody?*

She heard a small sound coming from the living room. She ran in, and there was Davey, her blond little beautiful brother, curled into a corner of the couch. He was weeping and rubbing his eyes, and his nose was running all over his face. He looked up at Gloria, and put out his arms to her. "Glory! Glory!" he cried.

She ran to the couch and gave him the hug of a lifetime. "I home alone," he sobbed, reverting to his baby talk. "I home all by myself. Mama not here. I scared."

She squeezed him and kissed his freckles, and smoothed his hair. "Oh, my poor little Davey," she crooned. She rocked him in her arms and hummed an ancient tune over and over. *For I have loved you so long, delighting in your company. Greensleeves was all my joy, Greensleeves was my delight.* The sweetly haunting melody calmed them both.

After a while he seemed ready to talk. Davey was regaining some composure, his six year old language returning. "I came home from school, and nobody was here. I thought Mama was out in the yard, but she wasn't. So I came here and waited. I was scared." He shuddered and started to cry again. Glory realized that Davey had been home all afternoon by himself.

"Don't worry, Davey. I'm here now. You're safe," she said. She picked her baby brother up and tickled his belly, and ruffed up his hair. She lay on the couch and lifted him high in the air until he finally started to laugh. "Weeeeee…you're a falcon flying high!" she exclaimed.

Glory looked at Davey's teary eyes, his red nose and face streaked with mucus. *I didn't know before how much I love you.* Just then, a glob of snot oozed out of Davey's nose, heading straight for Gloria's face. She tried to duck. "Yuck!" they both shrieked at the same time, hysterical with delight for each other.

Ma got home a half hour later, and heard the full indignant story from Glory of how Davey had been abandoned that afternoon and scared to death. "It seems to me," Ma countered, "that I asked you to come home from school straight away so I could get in a few hours overtime. I don't suppose you remember, rushing about the way you do." She turned to the sink and started to peel potatoes for supper. Ma didn't have to say much to get her point across.

Gloria felt so bad about disappointing her mother that she came home directly from school for the whole next week all on her own, and paid extra special attention to Davey.

And just for a while, she gave up playing her games with Mrs. Hansen.

After all, she realized, *now I finally understand why King Henry would give anything for a son.*

SUNDAY DINNER

There was this one time Ma got so angry, we all (Sammy and Penny too, not just me, I know I'm prone to exaggeration) thought maybe she was out to poison us.

Dad was visiting his sister, Auntie Miriam in the hospital. Ma was fed up with everyone. She had been in the kitchen all afternoon cooking and listening to everyone's complaints about what was for supper.

Even Dad had said before he left, "Will you cook that cow until it stops mooing?" It wasn't really a question. Dad wanted his meat cooked to the consistency of old shoe leather. Ma liked it blood red. *One would think that since she cooked the same things over and over, year after year, they could have figured out a way not to argue over it.*

But Herbie sometimes liked to tease and annoy his wife. He had left the house singing "O solo mio, spaghetti and meatballs!" Actually, he was thinking about his sister. He didn't want to show how worried he really was.

Ma watched him leave. She had a murderous look on her face. She slammed the roast into the oven, lit up a Chesterfield, and stormed into her bedroom. Being the rebellious sort, she knew it wasn't safe to smoke in bed, but she did it anyway. Smoking was Joyce's way of praying to the gods above that her sister-in-law's heart surgery went well.

Later that day, Sammy and Penny, who, having reached the mature age of seventeen should have known better, sat at the dining room table and looked suspiciously at the Sunday roast beef. They were wondering if this were to be their last day on earth. Ma had almost thrown their supper at them with a vile and withering look, and had retreated back to her bed to read the rest of the *Boston Globe*.

It's possible it's poisoned. I'm not eating it, they were each thinking. Sammy and Penny were twins, and they sometimes had similar thoughts. "Let's wait and see what happens when the peewees chow down," whispered Sammy to Glory. She nodded in agreement, and the three older children stared at their small siblings, watching to see if one of them keeled over or stiffed up, bug eyed in a high chair.

It would be just like Ma to trick us by feeding the little brats something different. She's only angry at us. It's maddening, really - Ma never blames the peewees for anything. They can do no wrong.

Meanwhile, Gloria felt she was called to task for everything, even the things she didn't do. *Like the time my whole class went on a field trip to Plymouth Plantation on the school bus.*

Glory didn't usually ride the bus. She had to walk to school, making this trip special and fun. She sat with her friend Beth. They did each other's hair into little braids on the way back.

There were kids making out in the rear seats. *I know them all and saw what they were doing, of course – how could you miss it?* But she hadn't kissed a boy since that peck on the cheek in fifth grade. *Besides, even if I had a boyfriend, which I don't, it would be gross to make out in front of everyone. Only the popular kids do that.*

The next day, there had been an editorial in the local daily rag of a newspaper with a screaming headline: "School Loses Control!" It went on and on about the kids in the back of the bus, and how the world was falling apart because of the lack of discipline. An old fashioned tirade right out of Bye Bye Birdie.

He's getting a little senile and starting to repeat himself. It's embarrassing to have parents in their forties. But Glory still laughed when her father responded to the idiotic waste of ink and newsprint by standing up with his arms widespread and singing out in his loudest voice, "Kids! What's wrong with these kids today?" *Once in a while, he can be funny, just a little.*

Ma, on the other hand, hadn't found the situation amusing. *She's a progressive, for crying out loud, with empathy for everyone else on earth.* A free thinker, so to speak, Ma didn't hold kindly to misbehavior from her own kids.

She encouraged you to have your own point of view on any subject, and showed real admiration for those of her children who could debate and defend their opinions vigorously. Glory had won solid points on many an argument, such as how the dinosaurs became extinct, or why we were in Vietnam in the first place.

But that was all in your head; your behavior was another thing altogether. Certainly kissing a boy was an infraction that, if caught in the act, would result in the ultimate in humiliation, a restriction of at least a week.

The offending article in the local yokel newspaper was rolled into Ma's hand. *I'm a bit surprised that Ma even read it, never mind take it to heart.* "Were you one of these kids kissing in the back of the bus?" Ma demanded to know.

"No Ma, it wasn't me, I didn't do it. I wasn't even sitting back there," Glory replied. *For God's sake, I won't play the persecuted queen.* "Why are you always blaming me for stuff I didn't do?" Her self-righteous tone bordered on whining, an offense that no one could stand.

Sammy said, "Oh, you're perfect alright! Miss goody two shoes." *Sammy could annoy the hell out of Hades. Always has to get in at least his two cents worth.*

Ma actually told him to mind his own business.

For either parent to correct the beloved Sammy is a miracle. Glory stuck her tongue out at her brother. *There'll be some sort of evil retaliation later, when I least expect it.*

Ma looked at Penny and asked, "Do you know anything about this?" Penny shook her head and looked down at the floor. She had just finished up a three week restriction for being caught smoking on the street. She wasn't about to say or do anything that might get her in trouble again.

"Are you sure you had nothing to do with this business?" Ma gave Glory that piercing inquisition style look that meant, I don't think I should believe you. There was something about Gloria, maybe it was the bombshell figure and deep, restless eyes that made everyone, including her own mother, doubt Gloria's innocence.

"Honest, Ma, I didn't do anything wrong." *And I hadn't, but nobody believed me.*

Her mother sighed and lowered the hand with the newspaper that had almost struck her daughter. She didn't believe in hitting. She picked up her cigarettes and matches and the nearest ashtray, and headed for the bedroom door.

~~~~~~

Glory looked over at Davey in the baby chair. Ma had cut his meat into little pieces to match the green peas and new potatoes on the plate. Suzi and Kit were old enough to use knives, but their food, too, had been precut like Davey's.

This is weird, none of them have gravy. Only we have gravy. Could Ma be that mad? Does she really want us to die? There was only one way to find out.

The gravy was dense and globbed up on the meat – Ma had used too much flour and not enough stock in the sauce. *A small amount of poison could be mashed into it without anyone being the wiser.*

Sammy took his fork and shoved it down into the brown goo. "Hey, you guys don't have gravy! Mmmmmm…it's yummy – want some?"

We've clearly hit rock bottom, the twins and I, luring our own tiny siblings to potential doom just to save ourselves. Glory knew it was wrong but couldn't help herself.

True innocents who hadn't a clue about life, the peewees adored their big brother and without hesitation took the bait. Sammy smeared his forkful on Davey's roast beef while Glory mashed up Suzi's new potatoes with the insulting brown stuff. *And Penny, our big sister who really should have known better, gave Kit a big lump of it right on top of her peas.*

No one likes peas, either frozen or canned - why Ma insists we eat peas, nobody knows. There were more peas under the table than ever landed in anyone's stomach.

The unknowing tots ate their supper with the suspect gravy, and it was soon clear they weren't keeling over. "More!" said Davey who hadn't had much lunch.

"How stupid are we?" muttered Sammy. "And now my supper's cold. It's all your fault, you moron!" he said angrily to the house fly buzzing at the ceiling fixture.

Later on, Dad came home and said Auntie was feeling just a little better. He seemed quiet and not in the mood for singing. He put his rare roast beef into a skillet and fried it up, the way he liked it. He didn't complain.

Ma came out of her room and announced to the kids that there was vanilla ice cream with sugar cones for dessert, a special treat. After a long, angry day, she seemed happier. She served up the cones and the kids took them out to the porch to watch the sun go down over the field.

Glory ate down to the bottom of her ice cream. She had only a couple of bites left when she saw several tiny colored sprinkles nestled in the bottom of the cone.

What's this? Ma had said nothing about candy sprinkles. Candy sprinkles would have been something to mention.

Glory looked at Sammy and Penny, and without a word between them, they sprang up and dumped the remainder of their cones into the trash. Their mother may not really have added poison to the ice cream.

She probably hadn't done anything wrong.

But they weren't taking any chances.

THE CARNIVAL

[Robin Hood and his merry men]

Kit and Suz weren't exactly twins, not like Sammy and Penny, but they sure acted like they were born from the same breath. Not that they looked so much alike – Suzi was a Gerber baby, round and angelic and pleasantly dimpled, with curly golden brown hair and twinkling eyes. She smiled a lot and moved old ladies to stop Ma in the street and exclaim, "Who's the darling in the carriage? What a beautiful baby!"

Kit wasn't quite so gorgeous to start. Always thinner than her year younger sister, Kit had a serious, drawn look on her face, and a strange unevenness to her mouth. With thick brown hair that was cut straight across and bangs with an edge as sharp as a knife, she didn't much love hearing about darling Suzi's baby curls.

But time has a way of fixing most things, and once Suz could walk just as well as anyone, Ma dropped the afternoon strolls with the carriage. Kit forgot the old ladies' remarks, and she and Suzi became the best of friends and quite inseparable. They ate together, slept in the same bed together, played house and fairies and school and Robin-and-his-merry-men under the pine trees together. Suzi liked playing Robin even though he was a boy. Kit was always Maid Marion. They had settled on it and stopped fighting long ago.

The girls gathered buttercups from the fields and Queen Anne's lace, and velvety pussy willows by the swampy sides of the road, and made tiny bouquets with ribbons to hang on their bedposts. They blew dandelion spore into the breeze, and pulled out the silky insides of cat-o'-nine tails to make soft beds for their dolls. Kit and

Suz shared a language that only they, and Ma sometimes, could understand. It was an idyllic existence such as the world rarely sees, living only in the minds and hearts of two very young sisters.

[Sir Billy's steel]

"Hurry up, will you?" Glory exploded at Camille. "Haven't you put on enough blush, for crying out loud?"

Camille eyed her best friend, and calmly continued her beauty regime. She was in no hurry to race out the door to the carnival. She knew Glory was always in a rush. But why? Mike and Billy would stick around, for sure, and wait for their dates to show up. It's not like they'd leave, thought Camille. Hell, they'd wait for us till the cows came home.

She brushed more pink on her cheeks, and chuckled to herself at the thought of poor lonely Mike standing by the cotton candy machine, staring at the gate by the edge of the field, watching for the cows, waiting for the love of his life to fly into his arms.

Her eyes teared up with laughter, and her mascara bled. It wasn't that she was mean, Camille assured herself as she dabbed at the black run with a tissue, just, not so needy. Mike was wicked good looking, the most handsome boy at school, and he drove a Mustang - which was almost as good as a Porsche. But he could wait, and if he didn't, there'd be plenty more love sick boys to take his place. Of that, she had no doubt.

Glory was at the end of her rope. "For Christ's sake, come on!" *It's true. I'm being unreasonable. Five more minutes won't make any difference.*

But she was nervous and wildly excited. Tonight was the night she was actually going on a date, and with the second best looking boy in the whole school. *Which isn't saying much because the vast majority of boys are idiots and morons without one iota of attractive quality among the entire lot. But Billy, he's a different story.*

Glory the Usually Bold was jerky and stupid and tongue tied around Billy. Every time he came near, she spilled her drink or made a lame joke, and it got so bad that she stopped trying to spit out even a word. She didn't know why, but this was the effect that Billy had on her.

So when Camille told her that she heard through Beth's best friend Patty that Billy told Mike he wanted to take Gloria out, everyone was surprised. Glory was awfully smart, that was a given. And pretty too (though no Camille) and funny and interesting in a strange kind of way. *But one of the popular crowd asking me out, and the second best looking boy in the school to boot? Something's up, something's very odd indeed.* Of course she said yes.

[Robin Hood and his merry men]

"Oooooh, what a pretty rock! See? It's got specks." Suzi and Kit were exploring the brook that ran through the woods, past the back of the baseball diamond over at the field. The brook had perfect, clear cold water, and a bottom filled with an assortment of granite pebbles, bird feathers, and the skeletons of tiny creatures. It was paradise for the peewees.

They practiced balancing right on the exact edge of the brook where the lady slippers and lily of the valley grew, where their bare feet stayed dry but the water ran by. Sometimes they missed if their foot hit a rock the wrong way, and then they got all wet and mucky. But it was great fun, and Ma never yelled at them for bringing home sand or mud or any kind of dirt.

In the spring, Ma would send them to the brook to search for fiddlehead ferns and wild chives, which tasted good cooked up with a little butter. And in the fall, the fox grapes ripened into purple concord grapes that smelled heavenly - smelled even better than they tasted. They were a lot of work to eat because of all the little seeds inside, but worth the effort.

Once in a while they'd go looking for mushrooms, but only when Ma went with them because, as Ma said, "Some mushrooms can make you sick. You never, ever eat a mushroom unless you show it to me first." Ma had read up quite a bit on the subject of mushrooms. The only time she ever ventured into the field was to help the peewees search for them.

Ma believed in freedom, but wanted to shield her children from the worst things in life, like eating a poison mushroom in the wild. Not eating mushrooms of any kind was okay with Kit and Suz, who could barf just thinking about them.

Suzi crouched down and picked up a wet shiny stone. "Ooooooh, here's another one! They're so much prettier when they're wet, don't you think?" she asked Kit.

"Yup," Kit answered, "but I like shells better. I like the kind that you hold up to your ear, and you can hear the ocean." Kit had had a serious infection in her left ear only the winter before, and lost some of her hearing. She thought a lot about ears and sounds and hearing and silence.

She was glad that her hair was straight and thick, because it covered up the spot where the surgery scar was. Kit was thinking, boy am I glad I don't have curly hair like Suzi's – I'd never cover up that ugly spot with her bouncy kind of hair.

At age six, Kit was finally outgrowing the odd looks of her toddler years and developing a real beauty. She knew it too, when she took the time to think about it. Which wasn't often, yet. Her world was full of too many interesting things. Like the mystery of how you could hear the waves in a seashell, even when the ocean was an hour's drive away.

Suzi said, "No, stones are definitely the most beautiful." Suzi was the direct type. She had her own mind, for sure, and wasn't afraid to voice her opinions.

[Sir Billy's steel]

They met up with Mike and Billy just as the sun set for good that night. The lights of the carnival glowed bright and garish. There was the Ferris wheel, the tilt-a-whirl, the fun house, penny arcades and shooting games, popcorn and candied apple stands, and at the back, pony rides and a merry-go-round for the little kids.

All the lights and sounds and people made Glory excited. *Like I'm in a different world. This cow town with all the dull and boring dairy farms - transformed into a city of light and sound, maybe like Boston or better yet, Times Square.*

Though Glory had never been to New York City, she could imagine what it might be. It was hard to believe that right across the street from her own house was another world, *a make believe place with lights so crazy bright they make the fields and woods around it dark enough to disappear into the night. Dark enough to make you forget they're even there.*

Glory didn't have much experience with dating. She didn't know if she'd be paying for her own rides. So she tucked her five dollar bill, birthday money, into her sneaker just in case. Glory wasn't one to save her measly weekly allowance – she spent it almost immediately on candy bars, Cokes, and red dyed pistachio nuts, items that her parents refused to provide.

The five dollars was all the money she had. It was a present from Nannie, whose traditional gift to each grandchild was a good amount of spending money and a pair of pajamas several sizes too big. They'll grow into them, was her motto. Nannie had lived through the Great Depression, and knew what it was like to have no money. She spent more of her pension than was wise on her beloved grandchildren, but even her own daughter Joyce couldn't talk her out of her generosity.

With the four of them together, Glory was having fun and not embarrassing herself too much in front of Billy. He treated her to fried dough sprinkled with cinnamon and sugar. *Commoners' fare, but tasty.* She managed to eat it without getting grease all over her smocked peasant shirt.

The mosquitoes were out – it was an especially bad season and the town hadn't yet sprayed the field. A huge one landed on Billy's nose. Glory slapped at it without thinking. Billy laughed and said, "We're fighting already?" He put his fists up like a boxer, said "Put 'em up – put 'em up!" and laughed some more. *He's actually kind of nice considering he's the second best looking boy in school.*

They walked around to the shooting games. Billy paid for Gloria's target shoot. She didn't aim it well and lost her shot. He paid for her to try again. *I don't want to look stupid. Besides, boys like to show off.* She said "Why don't you try instead? I'll bet you're pretty good at it."

Billy took her turn. Mike took Camille's and beat Billy three games to two. Then they rode the Ferris wheel in a car big enough for four, and saw the lights of the carnival from above. *Dating's fun, especially when you let the boy win the game.*

[Robin Hood and his merry men]

"Sammy," said Ma, "go over to the field and get your sisters, will you? It's almost time to eat."

Sammy mumbled on his way through the kitchen. "Why am I always the one who has to babysit those little twerps?" he said meanly. Ma gave him the glance and out he went, searching for his leather glove and ball along the way.

He crossed the street and loped through the gate. Sammy threw the baseball up as high as he could and caught it in his glove. That's about the best I've done this summer, he was thinking. There was no wind, and that helped. He was proud of himself; the ball must have gone six stories high at least.

He passed the carnival equipment that was set up to start that evening. "Wow, look at that! It's going to be so much fun tonight, I can't wait!" Sammy had six dollars to spend and he knew exactly what he was spending it on – the fastest rides on earth. Well, they wouldn't have a giant roller coaster like at Nantasket, but that was okay, he was going there later that summer anyway. This would be good enough.

Sammy hoped to see the love of his life, Denise, who had long red hair and looked great in tight sweaters. He was thinking, maybe if I'm lucky she'll take a little spin with me. He was only thirteen and had never actually kissed a girl, but he liked to think big.

He passed the baseball diamond and looked toward the tennis courts – no one there. It was lunch time and all the kids had gone home. Sammy strained to see if they were at the swings, then decided to check out the woods first. The peewees were probably playing Robin Hood in Sherwood Forest, down by the brook, their favorite place. Oh well, they were bound to be somewhere.

[Sir Billy's steel]

Soon enough, Camille and Mike split off and Glory was left with Billy. They took another ride on the Ferris wheel and shared some popcorn. *Billy doesn't have much to say,* Glory noticed, *and he isn't too smart. For God's sake, he's sixteen and hasn't even taken algebra yet. And he actually likes gym class.*

Even though he was the second best looking boy in school, she was starting to get bored. The money in her sneaker rubbed against her foot. The chafing made her limp just a little. Billy saw the limp and said, "Why don't we go sit over at the bleachers for a while?"

They walked past the merry-go-round and through the edge of the woods by the brook. Gloria got an odd feeling, and nausea swept over her. *Oh crap, I'm feeling sick to my stomach.* She'd never been much for the fast rides or the ones that go round and round, making you dizzy. *Maybe it was that popcorn. Stupid idiot.* Glory prayed to a god she didn't believe in. *Please, please don't let me throw up in front of Billy,* she exhorted the god with no name.

[Robin Hood and his merry men]

Glory was ten the last time she threw up in the field. The carnival had come to town, and Glory always delighted in the fact that it was right across the street. Even when she had no money to spend or it was too late and past bedtime, Gloria could always look out her window at the magic lights and merry sounds.

She had spent the day at Patty's. They had climbed the pear tree in Patty's back yard and eaten a couple dozen of the rock hard unripe fruit. Gloria ate so many of them that she barely touched the lunch Patty's mother made. *I can't be sick for the carnival. Must keep room for the cotton candy.* She came home right at five.

The carnival opened at six. It was five thirty and Gloria was anxious to get supper over and out the door. She had three dollars to spend that she had tucked into her Keds until she needed them. Ma said, "Why not wait and go with Penny later? I don't want you in the field today by yourself, Glory. There was a bad man in the field. The police are saying to be careful."

Joyce's philosophy was to allow independence generally, but to shield her children as much as she could from the really bad things in life. They'll learn soon enough, was her belief. She didn't think Glory needed to know all the details. She kept the worst to herself.

Nothing bad's going to happen to me. Glory said, "Oh, Ma – I'll be careful. And there are people over there already. I'll be okay."

Joyce relented. The man was probably long gone, she was thinking. Hitchhiked down the road and half way to Canada by now.

The lights weren't lit at the carnival when Glory arrived a few minutes later. It was dusk, and the mosquitoes were thick in the air. She batted at them as she walked around the fairground, noticing all the different rides and thinking about where she'd spend her money.

The carnival men were turning on the generators and testing the rides. She walked down to the end where the merry-go-round stood next to the woods. She leaned over the metal fence that surrounded the ride and admired the colors of the horses and carriages. *Royal purple, with blue and gold. That one's fit for a queen. Tally ho, my good man.*

"Hey girlie, you want a ride?" She looked up and there was the man who operated the merry-go-round. He was thin with a sharp face, and wore a dirty jacket and an ugly old army cap.

"I don't have a ticket," she said.

"That's alright, for a pretty little girl like you, I'll make an exception," he said. She hopped up and sat on the horse she had admired. *I'm the beautiful Maid Marion, riding to meet Robin Hood at the edge of Sherwood Forest.* The man started up the carousel and for her alone, ran the ride for a minute or two.

The merry-go-round stopped and she got off, smiling. *I wonder how many horses Robin stole from the rich to give to the poor?* She waved a thanks to the man and started for the popcorn stand. Seeing her leave, the man moved quickly to block her way. He took her by the elbow and said, "Well, ain't you got nothin' to say? Didn't you like the ride?" He was smiling strangely and leading her into the woods.

"Thank you," she replied, thinking that was what he wanted. *Ma taught me always to be polite, even to strangers.*

"I'll show you how you can really thank me." With one hand on her back and the other locking her elbow in his grasp, he ushered her quickly into the shadows.

Glory was confused. *Why is the man taking me for a walk?*

The carnival man pulled her under a big oak tree. He pushed her up against the broad trunk, and pressed his mouth on hers. Gloria had never been kissed before, not on the mouth. She froze and didn't speak.

The man rubbed his hands up and down the front of her shirt. He made strange sounds that Glory had never heard before. He pressed his body hard against hers, and the bark of the tree bit into Gloria's back. She felt his fingers against her pants, and then he forced her down to the ground. There was nothing about this that Gloria understood. *Except, this is wrong, really wrong.* She struggled but the man was too strong. She hit her head on a tree root and vomited as he came down over her.

Later, Glory walked past the cotton candy stand and watched a ring toss game. If you tossed your ring over a floating duck, you won a prize. She looked into the water and noticed her reflection. Her long dark braid was messed and halfway out of the elastic. *Did I forget to brush my hair today?* She saw her pants were wet and streaked with dirt and blood. *Did I fall? I don't remember falling.*

Gloria reached into her sneaker to get her three dollars. She wanted to play the duck toss. *Oh no, where is my money? I didn't spend it, did I? Maybe it fell out.* She wanted to cry. She had saved that money especially for the carnival, and now it was lost. She couldn't recall if she had gone on any rides. *Oh wait, maybe the carousel.* But it was all a blank. Honestly, she couldn't remember a thing.

[Sir Billy's steel]

Billy was insistent. If Glory was ready to puke, he didn't care. "Aw, come on," he said with a nasty whine. "You know why we came out here. Don't play all innocent with me."

So much for chivalry. I'm tired and I just want to go home. The bleachers are damp. My foot aches.

He pulled her toward him and kissed her with an ugly impatient passion. "Stop it, Billy! Cut it out!" she demanded. He wouldn't listen. He held her with one hand while the other pushed its way under her shirt to her bra. He shoved his hand under it and felt her naked breast. Gloria tried to pull back. *I didn't mean for anything like this to happen. I'm not ready for a boy like Billy.*

She slapped at Billy's face, and as she did, he suddenly let go. "No bitch is worth this!" he snarled. She fell onto the bleacher seat. She hit her back and tumbled down the steel steps to the ground. She lay on the damp dark grass.

Billy was infuriated. He said, "I only went out with you on a bet to see if I could get you laid. You'll never be popular. You're a joke, always in la-la land. You're probably a lesbian, that's what everyone says." Billy the Cruel walked away as though he were king conqueror of the world, back from a successful crusade. "I showed her," he announced to the dark field and hidden woods. "Must be a lezzie."

When he was gone, Glory pulled herself up off the ground and slowly limped through the field, past the diamond, past the carnival, past the gate, and home. She couldn't remember ever feeling worse.

Couldn't recall a time when she felt less like the queen she had always imagined herself to be.

She closed the bathroom door, and with a dull razor she found in the draw, cut fifteen slashes on her thighs and on her breasts. *One slash for each year of my failure of a life.*

She fell into bed exhausted with her Keds still on, the five dollar bill that started her blister and caused all her troubles still neatly tucked into her shoe. When she woke in the morning, the carnival had packed up and gone for good.

[Robin Hood and his merry men]

"Save me, Robin Hood, save me from the evil Sheriff of Nottingham!" cried Maid Marion. "He will take me to his castle, and I will be his prisoner. It won't be any fun, and I won't get to play in the forest or by the brook anymore. And he won't let me go to the ocean and collect seashells by the seashore. Please Robin! I need your help!"

Laughing, Maid Marion ran to the big oak tree and hugged its trunk, waiting for Robin to rescue her. She waited and listened, and waited some more. Where had Robin gone? It wasn't fair, he gets all the fun, she thought, and I just have to wait. She looked out at the open spot where she and Robin had been playing just a few moments before. She looked again - looked right into the terrified eyes of her sister Suzi.

Kit felt the world go silent. Something was wrong, really wrong. She could feel her heart jumping. Suddenly, someone was grabbing her arm and pulling her violently away from the tree. He spun her around and grabbed her shoulder with his other hand. His fingers were ripping her dress. Kit was paralyzed with fear. She couldn't move or speak.

From the opening in the woods, Suzi stared at the man with the dirty jacket and ugly old army cap. Her mother had told her never, ever to talk to strangers. She didn't try to talk. Instead, she let out a piercing scream that filled the air.

Sammy was on his errand looking for his sisters. He heard Suzi from across the brook. In an instant, he burst through the woods and lunged at the man attacking Kit. Sammy had the force of an arrow, flying straight as though it were from Robin's bow.

He knocked the man over onto the rocky ground and punched him twice in the head. "Get out of here, you goddamn mother f___er! Go away before I beat you to death!" he shouted. Sammy wasn't tall but he was fast and strong, and beside himself with fury, and determined that no one harm his precious little sisters.

The man hadn't bargained for a fight. He liked his prey vulnerable and unprotected and purely innocent. He stumbled up and ran off through the woods and out past the patch where the skunk cabbage grew.

Kit and Suzi rushed to their brother, and the three of them huddled together and wept. Even Sammy cried, though he would deny it later. He didn't bother to ask any questions of his sisters. He knew he wouldn't understand a word they were saying anyway.

They ran home holding hands as tight as they could hold. Ma called the police and reported a bad man in the field. Then they all ate lunch, and Ma, who usually let everyone fend for themselves at lunchtime, made grilled cheese sandwiches, everyone's favorite, to help calm down. She gave Sammy doubles plus chocolate milk from the farm, a special treat she had been saving for supper.

Kit had come to no physical harm, and after some time, both she and Suz forgot the man in the field. But they would always recall Sammy as a brave and noble knight, their defender who could do no wrong. And that was the last time Kit and Suzi played Robin-

and-his-merry-men. They knew they had a real hero in their brother, and didn't need to pretend that story again.

THE GRAY LADY

The night after she cut herself, Glory saw the Gray Lady for the first time. Not imagined, not pretended, not made up – the Gray Lady was real.

She was dressed in a grey gown from the Civil War era - stiff and tight at the waist, with long sleeves and full skirted. The Gray Lady had her hair pulled back and up in a bun. *She looks like a schoolteacher because she carries a stick or baton, or maybe it's a pointer of some kind. Everything about her, even her skin, is the same shade of steel grey. Her face is in silhouette.*

It was three or four in the morning the first time the Gray Lady appeared. Glory woke feverish from a strange dream. She dreamed that she and Penny were playing house under the pine tree. They were very small and young. They were having a tea party with all their dolls and teddy bears.

"Games first," Penny declared. She sang in her sweet soprano, "London bridges falling down, falling down, falling down..." They circled the bears over and over, and caught them in their arms, falling down laughing every time.

The dolls smiled. They were breakable and had to be handled with care. The game was fun, but they were ready for their snack.

"Have some tea, won't you?" Penny asked her nicest doll, the beautiful one with the curly red hair and ceramic face. "Oh, no thank you," the doll answered politely. "I don't drink tea. Do you have any cocoa?" "Of course I do, my dear," Penny replied, always the good hostess. "Let me get it for you."

Penny brought the pretend cocoa to her guest. As she leaned over to pour the hot drink, Sammy charged through the pine needles and knocked over the cup. The hot chocolate sprayed onto Penny's arm and scalded her skin. Penny began to scream.

She screamed and screamed until Ma and Dad came. They were both smoking their cigarettes; Ma her Chesterfields and Dad his Pall Malls. Dad said to Penny nastily, "Shut up! Shut your trap!" Ma added, "Why are you always whining and carrying on?"

They laughed at Penny. Glory and the ceramic faced doll tried to cover their eyes. *But we had to watch as Sammy took a cigarette and burned a hole in Penny's arm.* Penny stood in pain and mortification. Her bladder loosened and she wet all over the pine needle floor. Ma and Dad watched and laughed some more. "That Sammy, he's a riot," they said in complete and utter agreement.

Gloria woke up with a panic. *Oh God, what a horrible nightmare. It's not real, it's not real.* She tried to calm herself. Just then, the closet door next to her bed opened, and a ghost, all in grey, appeared from the dark.

She is floating into my bedroom. No, walking - well something in between. The ghost has a sternness on her face and a pointer in her hand. But she isn't menacing; she doesn't seem to mean any harm.

The Gray Lady didn't stop or look around. She didn't appear to notice the girls in the bedroom. She walked right past Gloria, took a turn at the bedpost, and passed by Penny sleeping in the next bed. Then she floated out of the room with a whispered wind-like tune. "Sur le pont d'Avignon, l'on y danse, l'on y danse…"

In the course of a few seconds, the ghost was on her way to someplace else. Glory was in shock. Her forehead burned. Her cuts felt razor sharp. *I don't believe it. I must be going off my rocker. In la-la land, for sure.*

Glory thought of all those kids at her school who take drugs, the ones who hang out downtown all day long doing nothing but hanging and smoking. There were a lot of druggies in her small cow town, more than the parents would ever guess. Glory herself had a stash of grass hidden in her bottom draw. It had cost her eight bucks.

She tried it only once, and it tasted and smelled more like oregano than pot. It didn't make her high. Maybe that was because she couldn't force herself to inhale. More likely though, she suspected she had been conned into buying a nickel's worth of plain old herbs. *I don't need it anyway. It's quite apparent I'm weird enough as it is.*

Three nights later, Glory saw the Gray Lady again. This time, instead of from the closet, she appeared from the dark front hallway. She walked straight through the bedroom again and out the other side. "Sur le pont d'Avignon, l'on y danse tout en rond." Though nothing else had changed from her first visit, this time the ghost seemed more than a strange curiosity.

She seems more than stern. She seems cruel, and she carries a menacing aura about her that makes me afraid.

The next morning, Glory snatched one of Sammy's baseball bats and propped it next to her bed. *I need to be prepared. Not sure for what. I am the most absurd person I know.*

She told Penny about the Gray Lady. Penny laughed for the first time in a long while. She told Sammy about Gloria's ghost. Sammy hooted with delight. "BOOOOOOOO!" he mocked. "I'm sooooo afraid!"

That night, Glory got ready for bed. She reached for the closet door. She had to get her nightgown that was hanging on the hook. She had to go to sleep, to take the chance of meeting up with her biggest fear, the Gray Lady. *Please let me live through the night,* she implored the gods of the underworld.

She braced herself and opened the door. Suddenly a body, stiff with death like an Egyptian mummy, fell straight out through the door jamb and smacked, face first onto the wooden floor. As though released from Hell itself.

Glory screamed with a fright that could burst her lungs. She screamed bloody murder. Through it, she heard a howling noise. It was coming from the corpse. Bravely, she opened her eyes and followed the unearthly cry.

It was Sammy. Though he had a bloody nose from where he hit the floor, he was laughing hysterically, wheezing and pointing his finger at Glory, yelling "Got ya!"

"You jerk! You imbecile!" Gloria screeched. She punched at him, and then she started to laugh. She was laughing and crying, and trying to catch her breath all at the same time.

Penny, who watched the whole thing from the hallway, came in and rolled on the bed, holding her sides and laughing so hard she started to pee. "Sammy, you're a riot!" she exclaimed, once her breath came back.

Glory was to see the Gray Lady float through her room many more times over the coming months. With each passing, she became more afraid – of the hallway, the staircase, her own bedroom, the closet. She began to feel dizzy in the hall and afraid to walk near the railing overlooking the stairwell.

But at the same time, she was getting used to her apparition, just a little. Even though she was groggy with sleep and afraid of the dark, Glory tried to stem her fear. She tried to be brave and look, actually look at the ghost as she passed. Glory began to wonder.

Why does the Gray Lady's face, always in silhouette, seem familiar somehow? The Gray Lady is starting to look like someone I know well.

The ghost has the face of Ma.

FRUITS OF THE SEASON

"Suzi!" Glory implored her small sister. "Dad says we won't go blueberry picking until everyone's gone to the bathroom. For crying out loud, go!"

It happened every time they crowded into their big old black Buick. A mile or two down the road, and Suzi had to go. *We'd have to stop on the side of the road, let her out, and wait.* Suzi would run through the weeds and wild flowers growing on the edge of the pavement, and into the woods. When she'd come back, Dad would take off with a roar. He couldn't stand little Suzi's tricks.

All that stopping and starting would make Kit sick. Her ear problems affected her balance as much as her hearing. Dad's jerky car movements made her dizzy and more often than not, she'd throw up out the car window. *It's a wonder we went anywhere together.*

But there wasn't a one of them who didn't love blueberries - blueberry pancakes with sweet maple syrup, delicate blueberry cake that was Ma's specialty, blueberry muffins, warm blueberry turnovers, and simply, fresh blueberries with pure vanilla ice cream. They were like a family of hungry wild bears when it came to blueberries, the favorite fruit of the late summer season. Today they were bringing every pot and large pan they owned to the pick-it-yourself blueberry farm in the next town over.

The only way they could afford the quarts and quarts of berries they'd consume over the next few weeks was by picking it yourself. Ma didn't can food or freeze much, as other women of her generation did. She preferred fresh fruit any day over canned. She was happy enough to wait until the season for the foods she truly loved. Like blueberries, butter & sugar corn on the cob, strawberries in early July, and crispy sweet apples in the fall. There was nothing like the taste of fruits in their season.

Suzi locked herself into the bathroom. She stood and waited. She hummed herself a little tune. "...Falling down, falling down, my fair lady." Then she flushed the toilet, turned on the water faucet, and let the water run a bit. She rumpled up the towel, came out and said, "Okay, I'm ready."

Dad said, "Are you sure you went?" He wasn't taking any chances.

Suzi was highly offended. "Of course I'm sure," she answered haughtily. Suzi wasn't lying. She was sure she went. She went into the bathroom, and that was the truth.

"Alright then, off we go."

They piled into the car, all eight of them, with four kids in the back. *Kit next to a window for safety's sake.* Dad drove, with Ma in the passenger seat as she never had learned to drive, Davey on her lap and Suzi up front in the middle. Even with all of them in, it wasn't exactly a tight squeeze – Dad didn't buy big black Buicks for nothing. Even Sammy, who would rather be out playing sports than in the car with the family, came along for the ride.

Penny sat next to her twin brother. It was a mistake. In no time, he began to flick his finger against Penny's knee. He knew it irritated her. Penny groaned and turned to look out the window. What an idiot, she thought. How did I ever get in the same family as Sammy? Sammy kept it up, flicking his middle finger with his thumb against Penny's knee. She tried to ignore him. Sammy wanted to rile her; he flicked harder and harder. "Sammy, cut it out!" Penny said.

Glory sat on the other side of Sammy. *I can't stop all the irritating and insulting things Sammy does to Penny.* She knew that over the years, Sammy had hurt Penny many times with his aggressive nature. She was his twin, but the mystical connection that often had them thinking the same thoughts didn't stop Sammy from being cruel to Penny.

He's bigger and stronger. Penny is weak. She's an easy target. It's not that Sammy is actually out to get Penny. At least Gloria didn't think so. *It's more like — she makes it so easy and can't put up a fight. He's athletic and super smart, difficult to fool. She's emotional and sensitive. Takes everything Sammy says the wrong way. You'd think that Sammy would be sick of picking on Penny. Our weary, tired sister.* But instead, it seemed he felt compelled to struggle on with her, to maintain his superiority and make sure everyone knew he was the brighter, the better, the stronger of the two.

Glory resolved to strike back. *Penny might not be Sammy's fighting equal, but I am. I'm just as smart as Sammy. And I'm not the least bit afraid of him.* She started to flick her finger on Sammy's arm. She flicked harder and harder until he stopped with Penny and turned his attention to her.

Gloria was just about to launch her next move when Suzi began to scream. "Stop — stop!" she cried. "I have to go. I have to go really bad!" She was hopping around in her seat.

Dad started to yell. "I thought you said you went before we left the house! There's no place to stop here!" Dad looked over to the side of the road. There was a sharp drop off into a ravine. The area was filled with nasty looking briars.

"I have to go, I have to go!" Suzi was frantic.

"Oh for God's sake, Herb, stop the car. It's better than letting her wet her pants," said Ma. She was just as annoyed as her husband. But having had six children and one miscarriage, she was more understanding.

Dad jerked the car to a stop, right in the road. It was a good thing they were the only car in sight. Then he started up with a roar, pulled over to the side, and stopped short again. He sat in his seat fuming. This is for the birds, he thought. Even blueberries aren't worth this aggravation.

Ma looked out the window. The drop off was steep at the edge of the road. She thought quickly. "Sammy," she said, "you'll have to carry Suzi down that incline. It's too steep for her."

"Are you kidding, Ma?" Sammy answered. "I'm not doing that." Sammy was mortified. He wasn't about to watch his little sister pee in the ravine.

"For Christ's sake, get out of the car, Sammy, and bring her down. Turn around while she's going, or close your eyes. Hurry up." Ma was no nonsense. She knew that Mother Nature is impatient; she waits for no one.

Ma opened the front door and Suzi scrambled out. She hopped around until Sammy got out the back door and lifted her up under her arms. With complete distaste he held her at a distance and raced her down the incline. Suzi sat in the nasty weeds, not a moment too soon. Sammy jumped aside and fell into a thorny patch. He turned his head and looked away while Suzi made her peace with Mother Nature.

"Okay Sammy, I'm ready," Suzi announced when she was done. Sammy stood up. His bare legs were covered in scratches. They climbed back up the ravine. Ma opened her door and Suzi hopped back into the front seat.

Just then, Kit pushed open the back door. She got it half way open. Sammy tried to step in while Kit was pushing her way out. She didn't quite make it. Sammy heard a terrible noise. It was Kit. She was throwing up all over him and the car door.

Ma laughed so hard she started to pee. "Sammy, take me down the ravine," she choked. Tears were rolling down her face. Sammy held his mother's hand as she worked her way down the slope. When she got to the bottom she told him, "Be a good boy, and get Dad to help me back up." You could hear her laughing all the way from the car.

Sammy scrambled back up the incline. He was on all fours, trying to get away from Ma as fast as he could. He put his hand down for balance, and shoved it squarely into a pile of animal dung.

"You gotta be kidding me!" Sammy yelled to the universe. He had never felt so humiliated. He was spattered with vomit. He had crap on his hand and scratches all over his legs. He took his tee shirt off and turned it inside out. With the dry parts, he wiped off his hand and the car door. Then he threw the shirt into the briar patch. It was a good thing the shirt wasn't a favorite anyway.

They all got back into the car and on their way to the blueberry farm. Glory and Penny, Ma and Dad chuckled the entire way. It was at Sammy's expense, but they couldn't help themselves. Gloria realized that the fight she had plotted for Sammy in her sister's defense wasn't necessary, at least not for that day. *Mother Nature stepped in instead. Her revenge is far sweeter than anything I might have planned.*

"There's the sign!" Kit said excitedly. She had recovered in full from her dizzy nausea spell and couldn't wait to fill her belly with all the blueberries she could eat.

They took the long dusty dirt road that led from the main street to the farmland a quarter mile in. They stopped at an old shack. It was one small open building with wooden fruit boxes and baskets and a stack of empty burlap bags set up on tables in the front.

The place had been whitewashed sometime in the past, but now was a peeling, sagging mess. There was a sign tacked to a post. It had been painted over and re-lettered many times in its long life. That day it said "Hansen's Farm – Peck tomato $1.25; Lettce 20 cents hd; Cukes 5 cents; Buttr & Sugr Crn 10 cents/$1 dozen; Maine Potato bag 40 cents Upick Blueberres FREE containers rbring yr own." It was the honor system – no one to know what you took or how much you paid.

Ma was indignant. "Ten cents for an ear of corn? Are they out of their minds? Just last week at Johanssen's, they were only a nickel." Their entire family loved fresh grown corn on the cob with tons of melted butter and covered in salt, though Herb had to cut it off the cob with a knife due to lack of teeth. Nannie liked summer tomatoes better than life itself, but still, there was no contest. Corn was by far the best vegetable of the season.

Ma figured that each of them would eat two ears except for the little ones, who'd eat one apiece. *Sammy could eat a half dozen if you let him. That boy has a hollow leg.* It was thirteen ears of corn for dinner, or a dollar ten with the discount. "It's highway robbery!" she exclaimed. She put a dollar bill into the coin box and carefully chose thirteen ears of corn. Baker's dozen, she thought. Close enough.

She piled the corn into one of the wooden fruit boxes. Herb put it in the trunk. These boxes come in handy, Joyce thought. She remembered how a few years back Herb nailed a fruit box to an old sled and pulled little Davey around the yard in the snow. Davey loved his ride and spending time with his father.

They had stayed out and played for quite a while until it got too cold and forced them in. Herb's circulation was never good. His feet hurt in the cold, a consequence of the touch of frostbite he earned while on guard duty during the war. He hadn't gone out in the snow with the kids for the rest of that season. It was just too painful.

Herb took the pots and pans out of the trunk. "Do you think they really mean the blueberries are free?" he wondered. "It's hard to believe they're free. Maybe they mean the containers are free." His repeating was exasperating.

"Well, it says the blueberries are free," answered Ma. "I'm not going to question it. You do as you please." Ma couldn't look a gift horse in the mouth. She wasn't about to assess the validity of the sign.

Each took a pot and moved out to the blueberries. They saw other families out in the field, some far off. The farm stretched for acres. There was no farmer in sight. The blueberries were the mid bush variety, easier to pick than the wild berries that grow low to the ground and you have to fight the bears for, but not so high that you couldn't reach the top. The bushes were just the right size. They were dripping with ripe blue hued berries.

Suzi and Kit held hands and raced to the nearest bush. They started shoving berries into their mouths. "Mmmmmmm, good," they shouted between mouthfuls. Penny took Davey's hand and together they found a good spot. Penny was judicious; she ate some and picked some berries for their pots while Davey force fed himself.

Ma and Dad, Sammy, and Glory found promising bushes and ate and ate, until they couldn't eat any more berries. The blueberries weren't the best, weren't the sweetest or juiciest they'd ever had. But in their frenzy, no one cared. They were the fruits of the season. Their family had waited so long for this moment to come, to taste summer's crowning glory, the mighty blueberry, everyone's favorite fruit.

Time went by. They ate and ate. Finally, their pots and bellies filled to the brim, they started back to the car. The pots were heavy and the kids started to complain. "Can't you carry mine for me?" whined Suzi. Dad had gotten over how Suzi had almost piddled in his car. He took Suzi's pot and told Sammy to take Kit's. Penny was already carrying Davey's pot. He'd eaten so many berries, it was only half full anyway.

They were most of the way back to the car when a family rushed past them, running with buckets filled to the top with blueberries. They gasped as they ran by, "The farmer is coming! The farmer is coming!" Ma and Dad looked at each other.

"So what?" they said.

"Those people picking next to us said the blueberries aren't free. The burlap bags are free. The blueberries are forty cents a bag!" they shouted on their way.

Ma looked at Dad, and they started to run. "Come on, kids!" they commanded their troops.

Glory and Sammy, Penny and Davey, Suzi and Kit all ran as though their very lives depended on it. The blueberries in their pots flew out every which way. Glory's pot fell and some of the berries spilled out. She stopped to pick them up, but Ma said, "They're lost to us now – keep running!" They ran as fast as their legs could tolerate, Sammy coming to the car first, of course.

Gasping for breath, they piled into the car with their pots of blueberries on their laps. Dad took off down the dusty road with a roar. Then he started to laugh, and Ma laughed too.

In an instant they were all howling with glee, holding their sides, trying not to dump berries onto the floor of the car. They hit the main road, on towards home. A minute later Suzi piped up. She couldn't hold it anymore. "Daddy, Daddy, stop the car!" she cried. Herb pulled the car over. He was laughing so hard he couldn't see to drive, anyway.

They got home with their stolen booty, and assessed the damages. Instead of eight full pots, they had five and a half. Not bad considering. We sure outsmarted that farmer, they all agreed.

"Gloria and Penny, shuck the corn, will you?" Ma instructed. They would have corn on the cob and hot dogs for supper. Ma took out bags of flour and sugar. She would make her delicious blueberry cake for dessert. "And rinse off three cups of blueberries for the cake," she added.

Glory took out a measuring cup and dipped it into a pot of blueberries. She pushed berries into the cup with her fingers. She looked at the pot, then she looked again. "Eeeeewwww!" she shrieked. She dropped the cup. The berries were moving. The pot was alive with worms.

There was no mistaking what had happened. They hadn't outsmarted the farmer at all. He had used the unwitting saps to clear his field of wormy berries. It was better than letting the birds get used to eating out of his fields. Short change me, will ya? Those city people, he chuckled. Don't know their arse from their elbow. They'll find out soon enough.

He was right. That night there was a lineup like you never saw at the bathroom door. They even used the broken toilet in the upstairs bathroom, figuring they'd deal with the damage another day.

But Mother Nature hadn't finished her vengeance. The next morning, everyone had sore bottoms from the effects of diarrhea. It was worse for Suzi and Ma, who had both stuck their bare bottoms into a patch of poison ivy down in the ravine. And for Sammy, whose scratches from the thorny briars and poison ivy blisters kept him humble for a whole week. Justice appeared to have been served.

There was only one thing you could say. Mother Nature rules. When she talks, you have to come a'running.

THE DUMP

It was the windiest Saturday yet that fall. Glory and Camille laughed together as heavy gusts pushed them along down the sidewalk. Her long hair, always wild and untamed, whipped across Glory's face and blinded her way. She pulled a strand out of her mouth and laughed again.

Autumn is without a doubt the best time of the year. I love the wind! And no goddamn snow, no sweltering heat, no mud, no bugs. Well, a few yellow jackets here and there, but nothing's perfect.

And the leaves – Glory had stopped collecting all the different colors and types of leaves long ago. When she was little, she layered her collections between sheets of wax paper and ironed them in, then tacked them up for display. She was way too old for that now, but always felt a rush of joy on seeing the autumn colors. *It's like Camelot, autumn – a fleeting moment in time, too beautiful to be real.*

She looked over at Camille, who was naturally thin and a little frail. Glory's build was wiry and strong for her height. Usually she'd be annoyed with Camille, just a little, for not being able to keep up. But today, Gloria was the one who had trouble meeting up with Camille, who was being pushed by the wind at such a rate as to make her run, not walk, toward the swings.

God, Camille is gorgeous. Why can't I look like that? Even with her chapped cheeks and fine hair all tangled up with the wind, there was no doubt that Camille was a real beauty, that kind of girl-next-door type with huge blue eyes and real, not bleached, blond hair. An inch or two taller than her friend, Camille had the face of a Guinevere and slim figure to match. Her destiny was written all over her. *Prom queen for sure.*

Glory knew that she herself was pretty. *Not in the fairy princess way like Camille. I despise pink and Camille always wears pink like some simpering, passive little baby ballerina. Pink is for wimps and princesses. Like Guinevere – save me, save me, Lancelot!* To give Camille credit, though, pink really is her color.

I'm different. I want to take space in the world. I'll be subject to no one. I refuse to be saved, by anyone, anywhere, any time. I wear purples and blues, the royal colors of a power to be reckoned with.

Vibrant colors are flattering on me. They bring out my violet eyes and black hair, make me look beautiful. She knew it, but she didn't always believe it was true. When they'd meet up with boys, every one of them would invariably first look at her chest, and then Camille's face. *Hello, I'm up here!* She never said it though. *All's not right in Camelot,* it occurred to her. *The queen is weak, just a pretty face. Any powerful woman is a witch.*

She wasn't about to give up her strengths for the sake of mere beauty. *Couldn't I have both?* Gloria wasn't sure about real life, but she knew it wasn't possible in Camelot. This was one story she'd never fit into.

But there has to be a happy ending - it's a goddamn fairy tale. She comforted herself with the alternatives. *I guess things could be worse. I suppose I could be downright ugly. Or flat chested. That would be the pits. A homely girl might inherit her throne, and the people would have to take pity and say, well she's no great beauty, that's for sure. But no flat chested girl ever won a queendom.* Of that Glory had no doubt. *There is no way the people would stand for a flat chested queen.*

They raced over to the field behind the school where the swings twisted in the wind. Glory and Camille loved the swings – they had a standing date every Saturday. *We'd meet downtown, buy a couple of Cokes and some pistachios or peanuts still in the shells, and head over to the playground to sit on the swings and gab for hours.* It was their time to be together, to be the young girls they were. *Not beauty queens or princesses or witches. Just us, free and powerful and alive.*

~~~~~

Penny helped Dad get the garbage ready for the dump run. No one liked going to the dump, but with such a big family, there was a lot of trash, and Dad hauled it in his big old black Buick every couple of weeks. He had loads of trash, enough to fill the back seat and the trunk.

Dad was paying Penny an extra quarter for allowance because only she was decent enough to help him that Saturday. Ma didn't do trash — it was a man's job; and besides, someone had to watch the little ones. Sammy was with friends, across the street at the football game probably, and Glory was somewhere, no one knew. So Penny, a mature and helpful daughter who could use the extra cash, offered to come with him to load and unload the smelly, dirty bags.

Davey wanted to come along for the ride, too. "Okay Davey, hop in the back," said Dad. Davey squeezed in next to bags overflowing with maple leaves they had raked that morning.

Joyously, he dumped leaves on his head. He was remembering how much fun it had been that morning to pile the leaves up high, then back up, get a good running start, and go flying head first into the pile. He and Kit had a blissful time, piling up the leaves over and over again. They flung themselves into the mountain of red and gold, covered up until they disappeared, and then called to Suzi, "Betcha can't find us!"

Suz was no fool — she knew exactly where they were. But the wind was stiff and leaves were blowing everywhere. The fun was starting to feel like work. She had her fill of leaves. She had abandoned their game and moved into the kitchen where Ma had made hot chocolate and deliciously delicate cider doughnuts. Kit soon followed.

Dad and Penny loaded the rest of the bags into the trunk, and with a plastic coated rope, tied it closed as best they could to the bumper. They went inside to use the bathroom. They ate doughnuts and drank down their cocoa.

After a time, Dad realized the day was passing. It was time to go. He drove with Penny next to him. She thought, the dump's no fun. But it's nice to be with my father. They didn't talk much. Dad was a quiet man who burst out into song when the occasion moved him, but lately all he could think of was his sister Miriam and the heart doctors at Mass General. He rarely spoke these days.

Penny was quiet too. She took after Dad in many ways, though she knew better than to sing. Like her father, her taste in clothes was never fashionable. *She wore orange, a color that only exaggerated her freckles.*

Penny had a few best friends and an almost pretty face with clear grey eyes. But being on the chubby side, she didn't get many invitations. That's okay, she thought, no one likes me but at least I'm not a loudmouth like my evil twin. And I'm not a nutcase like my ugly sister. She took some comfort in her thoughts. Penny knew that Sammy wasn't so much evil as aggressively opinionated and annoyingly boisterous. He really was smart and usually right. And Glory was so pretty – *she* was the ugly one, not Gloria. It just made her a little less sad sometimes to twist the truth around in her favor.

~~~~~~

They backed the car up at the dump site and began to unload the trunk. The edge of the trash heap was too far away to make the job easy. Dad moved the car up as close as he could to the burning refuse.

Trash was piled everywhere, and rats ran unafraid, burrowing through the mounds of garbage. The place stank. That morning, before the wind picked up, the trash man had started small fires here and there to help break down the piles. Now it was clear that had been a mistake. The wind was picking up little bits of smoldering trash, spinning them in the air, and sending sparks flying everywhere. The trash man was experienced with the weather, and wondering how he could have trusted that overpaid weather man to ever get the goddamn forecast right.

A spark landed on Dad's hand. He quickly crushed it and stood rubbing the sore spot. Another landed on his shirt and started to burn a hole in the sleeve. One caught in his hair. More sparks flew at Dad and the open trunk, then more. The bags caught too many sparks. Penny looked on helplessly as the trash in the trunk, and then the car itself caught on fire. "Penny!" yelled Dad, "Get back – get back! Get out of the way!" The trash man ran over with buckets of water. He and Dad tried to douse the flames.

Penny backed away from the car. She had never been so scared in her life. The thought of Dad with burns made her sick. She wanted to vomit. She wanted her father to take her away, to rescue her from the fire. All she wanted was to get away. Please save me, Dad, she cried to herself. She gagged on the smell of the burning tires.

Amidst the panic, she heard a small sound coming from the car. She looked over, trying to see through the smoke. She saw a sight no sister should have to see. It was Davey's screaming face plastered against the back window.

Penny heard an indescribable sound come from her body. In terror she raced to the car door. She pulled on the handle, but Davey had locked it from inside. Penny tore open the front door, reached back and pulled up on the back door lock. She ripped open the back door.

Davey leaped at Penny with a frenzy that almost knocked her

down. And then she ran, holding him for life itself, to the parking lot. It was only a fleeting moment in time, but she felt an eternity pass before they reached safety.

Herb heard Penny scream. He looked toward the terrifying sound, and for the first time in a very long while he lost his preoccupation. Herb really saw his family, the children he loved. He saw Davey, the precious son whom he had forgotten - had almost lost to the burning fire and his own neglect. And Penny, the loving daughter who, for no reason at all, he had taken so much for granted.

He raced to them with tears streaming down his face. "Oh, my wonderful boy, my beautiful girl!" he cried, hugging them with all his strength. He groaned and dropped to his knees, and thanked a god he had thought was dead. Behind him, the car burst into flames and was engulfed.

When Glory got home later that afternoon, everything had changed. An exhausted and hysterical Davey had been hugged and kissed more than all the other times in his life put together. He was allowed two cider doughnuts with his cocoa, and then had been promptly put to bed for a long nap. It was hoped that with sleep and attention, Davey would forget his horror story.

Dad was also in bed. The doctor was visiting. He said that Dad had a small stroke along with some burns, and needed rest above all. Dad was strong, he said, but a fright like that could kill a man.

And Penny. Penny was the most changed of all, but it was all on the inside. It remained to be seen how the events of the day would shape her life.

Meanwhile, Glory knew she had to thank her sister for the incredible deed she had done. She got out her best purple scarf, the silky one with the golden threads woven through. She presented it to Penny. *I anoint you forever more Queen Penny the Good.*

Penny cried. "Don't be afraid, Penny," Gloria said, trying to cheer her up. "You are strong and so brave. Nothing bad can ever happen to you again."

Penny shook her head. She didn't believe that what Glory said was true.

She took the scarf, but remained silent for the rest of the day and for days after. That night, she wet her bed. That hadn't happened since she was a child. She had to change all the sheets in the morning.

Gloria knew then that her power had failed. That in real life, no amount of saving or rescuing, no amount of wishing for a fairy tale ending could make it so. And though Glory wouldn't completely stop loving the autumn wind, she never laughed in its presence again.

KIT

Kit lay quietly, holding her breath so no one could see her under the pile of warm red and gold maple leaves. She counted to ten. "Ready or not, here I come!" she shouted. She jumped up and brushed the dead leaves off her apple green nightgown.

She looked around, half expecting to see Davey behind the tree. Davey was still young. He wasn't much of a hider. He thought that if he closed his eyes, no one could see him, even if he was standing right in front of you. Kit didn't mind – it was actually cute - kind of funny. She wondered if she had ever been such a baby.

Suzi of course was older than Davey, more experienced and better at the game. Davey must be with Suz, Kit reasoned. She couldn't find them anywhere. She looked up in the tree – not there.

She checked behind the wild corner at the fence where the bittersweet vines grew– not there either. Kit kicked at the pile of leaves where she herself had hidden. No one there. Where are they?

Kit searched her yard. She checked everywhere she could think they might be hiding. She looked behind the ugly hostas that grew and grew and needed cutting back. She crawled under the front porch and spied a silky spider web, but no sister or brother. She backed out from under the porch and ran to the clothes lines. Maybe they're hiding under a basket, she thought. But there were no clothes on the lines and no baskets in the grass.

"Where are you?" she called. No one answered. Finally Kit knew where Suz and Davey must be. They must have gone across the street, she realized. They must be hiding in the field.

No fair, Suzi! she thought with great annoyance. The self-imposed rules were clear even though they hadn't been stated at the beginning of this particular game. *No going into the field unless everyone agrees in advance. That was the rule. Everyone knew it, even Davey. Their yard was the limit.*

Kit always played by the rules. She liked rules – rules made everything fair, and fair was more fun.

You didn't have to worry about Kit. Kit was careful and stayed within the lines. You could count on her – you didn't even have to ask her where she'd been because you knew she'd been good and reasonable, and had stayed safely within her boundaries. Ma never needed to know where Kit was.

Suzi was different, a freer spirit. She didn't care about her outside limits as long as she was having fun. She got bored with the rules and forgot about them soon into a game. Today was no exception.

Kit started out for the field. She was careful at the busy road. She knew her left ear didn't hear so well. She looked one way, then the other, waiting for the cars to zoom by. When all was clear, she crossed.

The pavement was cold on her bare feet, much colder than the grass in the yard. She started to shiver as she walked through the gate and into the field. I should have taken a sweater, she thought. I should have worn some shoes.

"Where are you? You're not playing by the rules. Where are you?" Kit called into the empty field. She turned her good ear toward the swings that were way over the other side, near the school.

She thought she'd hear Davey with his high soprano voice singing "Daisy, Daisy, give me your answer do. I'm half-crazy all for the love of you."

She figured for sure she'd hear Suzi with her piercing Ethel Merman voice bellowing out "Kids! What's wrong with these kids today? Noisy, crazy, sloppy, lazy, loafers…and while we're on the subject, kids!"

But she heard nothing.

Kit hobbled across the stone drive. "Ouch, ouch, ouch!" she shrieked. Each step took another bite out of her cold, unprotected feet. Shivering, she walked to the bleachers. Not under here, she observed. Where could they be?

She climbed up to the top of the frosty steel steps, calling, "Davey! Suzi! You're not playing fair!" She looked across to the brook. Not there.

She looked past the fence at the baseball diamond. Not there either. Now Kit was mad. She was all alone and no one seemed to notice. "Suzi, it's not fun anymore! I'm here. Don't you care? Doesn't anybody care?"

Kit stood on tiptoes and strained to see the swings, strained to hear her brother and sister singing their usual happy refrains. She leaned over with her good right ear to hear their sounds, and fell, headlong, down the flight of frozen steel steps to the ground below.

~~~~~~

Glory awoke with a start. It was pitch black in the bedroom, the middle of the night. Freezing cold.

She heard a sound. A high pitched noise, a shrieking sound coming from the upper hallway next to her room. She picked up the baseball bat that was leaning next to her bed. "Penny," she whispered. "Penny – wake up! I hear something."

Penny groaned and turned over. Her weird sister Glory was at it again. The ridiculous Gray Lady, she thought. This is getting out of hand. "Glory, go back to sleep," she said. "You're just having a bad dream." Penny thought, I can't wait for next year when I'm off to college and out of this nut house forever. I'm gonna leave and never come back.

Glory lay back into bed. Penny's right, she thought. It's not the first time I've had a dream bad enough to wake me up. She tried to remember. It was funny but she couldn't recall having a dream. Her hand relaxed around the baseball bat. She was leaning it back against her bed when, there was the noise again.

This time, Penny heard it too. She bolted upright. "Glory, turn on the light," she commanded. Gloria reached for the string that connected to the bare bulb on the ceiling. She pulled on it. The room flooded with a glaring, blinding light. She shielded her eyes and reached for her bat. It's about time Penny took me seriously, she thought. Now who's the crazy one?

Glory swung her legs off the bed and stepped onto the icy cold wooden floor. "Ouch, ouch!" she cried. "It's freezing in here." It must be the Gray Lady, she reasoned with herself. I've heard that ghosts leave cold trails behind them.

A shrieking, high pitched howling sound came whistling down the hallway. Glory froze.

Penny was filled with dread. The last time she felt so afraid, her little brother Davey was caught in their burning car. She remembered his face, the screams she saw but couldn't hear through the glass of the windshield. She had prayed to the mother within her never to witness a sight like that again.

She prayed once more. Please let this be only the wind, just the sound of the winter wind through a pane of broken glass. Penny prayed, but she didn't believe there was anyone listening to her prayer. She grabbed the bat from Glory's grasp, and prepared to protect them both from whatever loomed in that dark, cold hallway.

Penny and Glory crept slowly toward the door. They got to the door jamb. Another howling sound came from the dark. Penny bravely thrust her hand through the opening, around the corner, and switched on the hall light. Their eyes adjusted, and with the bat raised high, they stepped through the doorway into the hall.

There was Kit in her apple green nightgown and bare feet, walking over the cold maple floor of the hallway. She was asleep. Her eyes were closed but she was talking, howling something. Something like, "I'm here, I'm here!"

Kit took a small step. Her foot hung over the top of the stairs. She leaned forward, shrieking, "Don't you care?" She paused and turned her head to the left, as though listening for an answer.

Penny had seen Kit sleepwalk before, and knew she must be careful. You never try to wake up a sleepwalker, she'd heard. They'll go crazy. But Penny also knew she had no time. Because Kit was perched on the edge of the stairs.

She streaked down the hallway and lunged for Kit. But it was too late. Kit leaned too far. She lost her balance and tumbled down the cold wooden steps to the landing below.

~~~~~~

Kit woke up and started to cry. I'm all alone, she wept. Where's Suzi? Where's Davey? I'm scared. Where's my mama? It's not fair — I play by the rules and they don't. No one cares where I am. No one cares what I do. Tears streamed down her small face. She was broken hearted. She felt all alone.

~~~~~

Penny woke up with a start. Tears streamed down her face. Her little sister Kit was dead, in a heap at the bottom of the stairs. She couldn't save her. She had saved Davey but she couldn't save Kit. Penny was heartbroken. She knew she would never be good enough, not for this family with their high expectations.

But she couldn't save everyone – how could they expect it of her? She was only a girl herself, not a queen or anyone's mother. I'm not Penny the Good, she thought. Not good or brave or strong. She hated her family for imposing this burden. Hated herself for her inferiority, for not being able to live up to their ideals.

Then she heard a sound. It was a high pitched howl coming from the hallway. Penny listened. She heard it again. Someone was crying.

She got out of bed and tiptoed past Glory asleep in the next bed. She turned on the light in the hallway. The floor was icy cold. She heard the cry getting louder.

She followed the sounds into the bedroom where the peewees slept. There they were, Davey asleep in his cot, Suzi sound asleep in the double bed she shared with Kit. And there Penny found Kit, perched on the edge of her bed, crying as though her whole world had ended that night.

In seeing Kit, it was as though a great weight lifted off Penny's shoulders. She had never, ever been so happy to see her tiny sister. She held out her arms to Kit, who was miraculously unhurt and alive and safe. She gave her the hug of a lifetime.

Rubbing her eyes, still waking from her dream, Kit cried, "Penny, I'm all alone. No one cares about me. I could be dead and no one would even notice."

Penny didn't know why Kit felt this way or why she said the things she said. They were Kit's feelings, and couldn't be denied.

But she knew that Kit was wrong. There was at least one person who cared that she was alive. She was not alone.

Penny stroked her small sister's teary cheeks. She rocked her back and forth and softly hummed a favorite tune. *"Greensleeves was my heart of gold, and who but my lady Greensleeves?"* She sang the words over and over, calmly and sweetly, until Kit returned to the bliss of a young girl's deep sleep.

Then Queen Penny the Good closed her eyes, and slept like a child until the morn.

THE OAKS

Glory stared hard out the classroom window at the driving sleet pounding the oaks in the school yard. *Serves them right. Those oaks are so haughty and stuck on themselves.*

The oaks had lived in that same spot for at least a couple of hundred years, Glory knew. Only a truly fierce wind, like a hurricane, could bring them down. And by November there was no chance of a hurricane in southeastern Massachusetts.

This nor'easter was just a tickle to the mighty oaks. No amount of sleet could tear away more than a few sickly branches. We've made it through another season, they seemed to say, taunting Glory. We're here for good, whether you like it or you don't - you little intruder, you newcomer, you nobody.

I'm not a nobody.

You oaks are mighty, it's true. You're ancient. But I've been here almost sixteen years. That's a good long time. And guess what? Mother Nature rules, not you oaks. She bears watching. She could dry you up and shrivel your acorns. She could hatch a million squirrels to eat every nut with none to seed. She can set a lightning bolt on you faster than you can say Thor's thunder. I know I don't have a perfect relationship with her, but neither do you.

Glory took some satisfaction in her thoughts. *What wind velocity could bring down an old oak?* She began the calculation in her mind.

"Miss M____, are you with us today?" Mrs. Standish asked impatiently. It was the standard teacher inquiry for those not paying attention. A sarcastic put down without the actual words being demeaning. I'm only asking for a simple explanation of the properties of wind, the teacher thought. A prime relationship, a simple formula. Is that asking too much?

Madeline Standish was devoted to her sophomore honors physics students. But even her top students could, at times, try her soul. She'd caught Gloria day dreaming too many times already this year, and it was only November. Glory had changed, becoming more withdrawn and less interested in the class.

Madeline wondered how the brightest star of her ninth grade biology class could be so disaffected by physics. Which subject is, as everyone knows, a higher calling. She was determined to find a way to pull Glory back to a love of her favorite subject. Even though, she was quite aware, science isn't so important for girls, not even in this modern world of 1968.

She thought, Glory won't need physics for a life on the stage, playing the great Elizabeth. Or Mary Queen of Scots, or Ophelia. Glory's headed for the stage, that's clear. Still, there's the question of pride in my work. Glory won't make a fool of my teaching skills. She won't jeopardize my standing on the faculty. No matter how smart, she won't intimidate me. Madeline was determined.

"Sorry, Mrs. Standish," Glory responded with actual sincerity. "I was only trying to figure out the wind velocity needed to bring down one of those old oak trees. I know that sleet by itself doesn't have enough mass. Even a heavy wet snow wouldn't do it."

Madeline took in a long breath and silently thanked her god for the positive response. Glory was a leader in the class and could lead the others astray. She reacted kindly.

"That's an interesting application of our lesson, Gloria. Let's look at the variables in this case…"

The class groaned. Glory was making a sap of Mrs. Standish

again. Likely lost in her fantasy world. Probably pretending to be Maid Marion, meeting up with the love of her life, Robin Hood. Glory the Weird, but smart enough to get away with it.

The bell rang, and the physics students raced out the door.

"Stay a minute, will you, Gloria?" Mrs. Standish asked.

What's important enough to make me late for my next class?

Madeline looked at Glory. She saw a vibrant girl with a movie star figure, startling violet eyes, and wild dark hair strung with colored beads. Those hippies, Madeline thought, out to change the world. Our perfectly good world.

"Miss M_____, you simply must pay more attention in my class. Your grade depends on it. You want to go to college, don't you? Well, of course you do, a bright girl like you. Not that girls need college. But you don't want to end up a nobody, do you?"

I'll never be a nobody.

Glory drew herself up out of her self-indulgent slouch. Her eyes turned dark and piercing. She looked at Mrs. Standish with the wrath of the high born.

I am Elizabeth of England, the great queen, and being spoken to as a lowly sailor.

Madeline sensed she had said the wrong thing. She tried again.

"Glory, as a member of God's Chosen People, you have a special obligation. You have to try your best. We know that all Jews are smart. That's God's truth. God expects a lot of you."

Oh, is that all this is?

I'm not about to let on to Mrs. Standish that I don't believe in the god of the Jews. Or any other god for that matter. And as for having high expectations placed on me, well, Ma takes on that role just fine.

"I promise to try harder, Mrs. Standish," Glory replied to end the conversation. "But I have to go – Mother Nature calls." She blushed and ran out the door to the girls' room down the corridor.

She's complicated and interesting, Madeline admitted to herself. But Jews are tricky. I much prefer our normal girls. Still, I treat everyone the same and I'm proud of that. It's a modern world, after all.

She drew up her papers into a neat stack and erased the formulas on the board. It's potluck tonight, she remembered. Descendants of the Mayflower night.

She looked out the window. Hope this blasted sleet doesn't cancel our meeting. The difficult season is upon us. But I pride myself as a true Yank, and a little bad weather won't change my plans.

She thought of the pickled cabbage dish she'd be bringing for potluck. It was the same dish she'd been making her whole life, following Grandma Prissy's recipe. Her friend Helen, the home economics teacher, had suggested adding a pinch of cinnamon for excitement. But Madeline was unmoved. No need to change a thing, she thought with unbending conviction. It's perfect just the way it is.

SUZI AND THE BLUE FAIRY

Suzi turned over in her bed and tried to get comfortable. She couldn't sleep. She kicked at her blankets. She lifted her pillow and turned it over to get to the cool side.

The air in her room was sticky and hot, and Kit was breathing loudly. Suz pushed Kit over to make the sound stop. Kit grumbled something in her sleep and turned on her side, away from her sister.

The boards under the bed frame, the ones holding up the mattress, were cracked in the middle. When Kit rolled over, Suzi fell down into the middle of the bed. She was hot and annoyed and stuck like Pooh Bear. She struggled her way back to her side of the mattress. This was going to be a long, long night.

She got out of bed, tiptoed past Davey sound asleep, and sneaked over to the door to Sammy's room. She pushed the door open enough to fit through. The door made a terrible squeaking sound that Suzi was sure would wake everybody up, but no one moved. She sneaked over to Sammy's bed. "Sammy, wake up, wake up!" she whispered.

Sammy had been sound asleep. He was dreaming about riding the giant roller coaster at Nantasket Beach. He'd been flying through the air feeling enormously powerful, omnipotent, like Superman. He was like a speeding bullet. At the dizzying top of each hill of the giant ride, seconds before the screaming descent, he could look out across the ocean and see the islands of Boston harbor.

One of these days, he was dreaming, I'll fly right off and see the world, everything there is to see on the other side of those islands. Sammy wasn't sure what he wanted to do after high school, besides go to college. Whatever it turned out to be, it would be supreme, the best, the fastest, the highest, the smartest. Of that he had not the slightest doubt. He would shake loose from his old cow town. He would show the world his stuff.

When Suzi walked in, he woke up with a start. Sammy was irritated that his nine year old sister had brought him back down to earth with such a thud. "What's wrong, Suzi?" he asked in a sleepy, cranky voice.

"Nothing's wrong. Why do you think that?" Suzi asked. *One thing about Suzi, she knew her own mind. She knew what she was all about. There was no messing with Suzi.*

"Ugh! Go back to sleep!" Sammy turned over and pulled the blanket over his head.

"But Sammy, tomorrow night we're getting presents. It's the first night of Chanukah. We'll be turning on the blue lights. I can't sleep – I'm too excited!"

Suzi danced around on her toes. The floor in Sammy's room was icy cold. It was made of maple wood and didn't have a carpet on it like Suzi and Kit's room.

The old house, built thirty years before the Civil War, had one hot spot - the peewees' room, and many freezing cold places. Suzi and Kit never had to suffer, as we older siblings did, the long cold winter in rooms that could freeze your breath.

Sammy knew what it was like to be so excited. He remembered the year he got a fancy new sled that moved like the wind down the hill on the other side of the field. It was the best gift he'd ever received.

Ma and Dad gave Chanukah gifts only on the first night of the holiday. There was no way they could afford to give their six children gifts for eight nights straight as custom demanded. Each child got one big gift and two small ones, usually clothes; no more, no less. It was the only Jewish holiday that Ma allowed, and then only because Christmas was so big in their town.

Ma allowed her kids belief in Santa Claus too. Each got to nail up a knee sock to the fireplace mantel. It would be filled with an orange, an apple, several walnuts still in their shells, a candy cane, some loose chocolate candies, one or two small toys, and a few pennies. And Chanukah gelt, gold foil wrapped chocolate coins. *No doubt to assuage the guilt of giving in to Christian ways.*

But as soon as one of the kids learned that Santa wasn't real, that would be his or her last year for a visit from jolly old Saint Nick. This Christmas would be Davey's last time to put up his stocking. At age six, he had already heard in first grade the news about Santa. *You couldn't fool Ma into giving you extra years. She knew when you knew the truth.*

"And I know what I'm getting this year," Suzi announced excitedly. She flapped her arms like a bird and twirled around and around. Suzi was plump but very light on her feet. "An Easy Bake Oven! That's what Kit really wants but I think I'm getting it instead."

She danced around the small bedroom. To Sammy, who had gotten past his irritation, Suzi looked like a little fairy princess with her billowy pale blue nightgown and shiny, golden brown curls.

"Wouldn't you rather have it be a surprise?" he asked.

She answered matter of factly. "Yes, it's true I like surprises. Oh, I wish, wish, wish for an Easy Bake Oven, but maybe a surprise would be better."

Suzi yawned and stretched her arms. "I'll go back to bed and wait for a beautiful surprise tomorrow night. They'll be chocolate coins, and presents, and blue, blue lights – the bluest of the blue. G'night, Sammy."

She turned on tiptoes and floated back to her room. She fell into bed and was asleep in an instant, dreaming all in blue, her favorite color.

Sammy tried to return to his Superman dream, but instead, he lay awake wondering what his Chanukah gift would be this year. He would have liked a new baseball glove, but figured his parents would be practical. It would probably be a suitcase, one big enough to take him out of this cow town, off to college next fall. Sammy closed his eyes. Yup, he thought, that will be more than good enough.

~~~~~~

Suzi's blue dream was more than a dream. It was a remembrance of some much younger days; a recollection of a time when she was only four and Kit was five years old.

"Hurry, Kit! You don't want to be late!" Ma called up the stairs. "Not on your first day of school! Glory, come on – you too!"

Why do I have to walk my little sister to school? Glory wondered. *It's absurd – I'm in fourth grade, the oldest in our elementary school. Kit's only starting kindergarten. It's going to be really and truly embarrassing, showing up at the school ground with Kit in tow.*

But she didn't argue with her mother. *There's no winning. Well, maybe I'll ditch Kit at Birchwood Street,* she plotted meanly. *It's only a couple more blocks from there. If she can't make it that far herself, she's too much of a baby to be going off to school.*

Glory looked in the mirror at the dressing table in her room. She wore a new dress for the first day, the only new dress she'd get that year. It was a striking deep forest green with cap sleeves and smocking at the top interlaced with lilac colored ribbon.

Penny had tied a matching bow into her hair. *I love my new Shirley Temple dress. And my hair isn't too frizzy. Even Elizabeth herself would approve.* Glory was anxious to start back to school, though she'd never admit it. She had been bored, more than a little over the past few weeks, waiting for summer to be over.

In her favorite color red, Kit had a new dress too and looked perfectly groomed. Wearing only hand me downs from older cousins, she had never owned a brand new dress. It resembled Glory's in style, but hers had tiny white buttons down the front and on the edge of the sleeves, and a pattern of small white roses on a field of deep red. Kit had a red ribbon in her hair, white ankle socks, and black Mary Janes. She felt divine.

Kit was nervous and excited, and ready for kindergarten. She picked up her satchel that held her school supplies, all new. There were crayons that no one but she would use. Not Suzi who, with an awkwardness that came from being left handed, always pressed down too hard and broke perfectly good crayons. And not Davey, who was so babyish he put the crayons in his mouth and then spit out little pieces all over the floor.

Her eyes sparkled as she thought about all her new possessions. Besides crayons, there was a pencil box with three newly sharpened pencils, an eraser, and a small ruler. She had a notebook to write in, two wrinkled but clean handkerchiefs, and an apple for a snack.

Kit felt pretty and grown up, not a baby any more. She stood by the back porch and waited for Glory. A minute later, they were out the door and on their way.

Suzi stood at the door and watched her two sisters walk down the street in their lovely new dresses. Suzi had never had a new dress, one that she was the very first to wear. All her clothes came from her sisters, most of the dresses from her older cousins.

Usually she didn't think much about what she was wearing or fancy clothing, but today was different. Suz thought, I would look like a fairy queen in Kit's dress, especially if it were blue. Blue is so much prettier than red. Yet she had to admit that Kit's dress, and Glory's too, were the most beautiful she'd ever seen.

She waved to Kit, but Kit didn't turn around. She called out "Kit, you're so lucky to be going to school! Goodbye, Kit!" but Kit was out of earshot.

Suz watched until she couldn't see them anymore. She felt a loneliness she had never experienced before. Her best and only real friend, her dearest sister Kit had just walked out the door without even saying goodbye.

She started to cry. She didn't want to be stuck playing only with Davey. Davey was a baby who could barely walk straight. You couldn't really play with him. She wondered what she would do all day long without Kit. She didn't want to be all alone with nothing to do.

She felt sad, and then she got mad. She had a strong determined mind, and as the reality set in, she grew beside herself with fury.

Suzi ran into the kitchen where her mother was drinking her morning coffee. "Mama! I want to go to kindergarten, too!" she cried. "Why can't I go, too?" She exploded into a rage. She lay on the linoleum floor and kicked and screamed. She threw a real fit, a bona fide tantrum. "I want a new dress! I want to go to kindergarten like Kit! I want new crayons – mine are all broken! Why can't I go, too? I want to go to school!"

Joyce sipped her coffee and watched calmly as Suzi beat the floor with her fists. It is a well-known child rearing practice, Joyce was thinking, to allow a child to express her rage until she exhausts herself, until all the anger is spent. Then, put her to bed for a nap and when she wakes up, all will be back to normal.

She considered picking Suzi up and giving her a hug. She knew, after all, that Suzi had just lost her best friend in the whole world, her constant companion. It was natural for a small child to have no understanding, no sense of why Kit was going off to school, or even what school was. She had a great deal of compassion for Suzi.

Joyce remembered how her own small sister Sadie was treated whenever she had one of her fits. Her grandmother Bubbe had no tolerance for tantrums. Whenever Sadie misbehaved, Bubbe would pick her up kicking and screaming, and lock her into the dark corn bin in the basement of their tenement building. Sadie, as young as three years old, would have to wait there until either Bubbe thought she had had enough punishment, or Bubbe knew Mama was soon coming home from work. Joyce never dared to intervene.

That's why Aunt Sadie is the way she is. Angry and unhappy, distant and sometimes cruel. Mentally ill, really.

Joyce had compassion for her sister, and no intention of taking after Bubbe in the raising of her own children. She would do her best to give them freedom to express themselves, license to explore the world, opportunities she never had, a life free from violence. Joyce seldom thought to spank her kids or to punish them beyond reason.

But she kept her distance. Something in her stopped short of acting on her compassion, of showing physical warmth or love toward her children. Perhaps it was because she herself hadn't experienced it, or couldn't remember when she had. For whatever reason, beyond the baby stage, once they had personalities and speech of their own making, Joyce couldn't hug or kiss her children. She couldn't tell them they were wonderful or even good. She couldn't mother them in the traditional sense.

The best she could do was to let us work out our problems in our own way, in our own good time.

To give Joyce credit, Suzi was not in a huggable state. So Joyce let little Suzi kick and punch the floor and cry and scream until she lay exhausted in the kitchen. The whole ordeal lasted over an hour.

When she was done with her fit, Joyce carried her small daughter up to bed for a long nap. Suz will be fine when she wakes up, Joyce thought. I'll make some cocoa and help her cut out paper dolls. And then Kit will be home from school. After all, kindergarten was only a half day – Kit would be back by lunch.

Suzi did have a long sleep. She slept all that day and into the next. Joyce worried, but thought it best to let Suz rest. When she woke, she seemed fine, just as Joyce thought she would be. "Would you like a peanut butter and jelly sandwich and a glass of milk?" her mother asked her.

Suzi was hungry. She hadn't eaten since the day before. She replied, "Yes please, and would you make one for my friend, too?"

"What do you mean, Suzi? What friend?"

"My blue friend – the Blue Fairy. She's sitting right here, can't you tell? Isn't she pretty? She's hungry too."

Suzi turned to her left to talk with her invisible blue friend. She was full of news. "Blue Fairy, we're going to have so much fun today. First we'll go swing on the swings. Then we can have a tea party. Yes, you can bring Teddy. Then we'll play hide and seek. How do you hide with those big blue wings? I'll bet I can find you right away!" Suzi started to laugh. She and her new friend were going to have a glorious day.

Joyce was stunned. She quickly lit a Chesterfield and drew in a long breath of smoke. She didn't know what to think or how to react. She prayed to her cigarette god for guidance.

In the end, on the surface of it, she did nothing. But the real truth was, Joyce let Suzi work out her problems in her own way, in her own good time.

The Blue Fairy became Suzi's instant best friend. They were inseparable for an entire year in their highly selective Blue Fairy School.

When Suzi went off for real to kindergarten, within a week of starting school she lost the need for her imaginary friend. But though she wasn't visited by the Blue Fairy anymore, Suzi remembered her quite fondly as the loyal friend in blue who saved her from her own loneliness. And Joyce breathed an enormous sigh of relief for the happy ending to this story.

~~~~~~

Sundown finally arrived, and with it the first night of Chanukah. There were no prayers, no singing, no dreidels. Not even real candles or a real menorah. Ma was firm about no religion in the house, ever.

So much so, I thought candles were for only for Christians. I went to a Catholic church once and saw people lighting candles and putting coins into a box while saying their prayers. I didn't know that Jews light candles every Friday night.

Glory and her brothers and sisters didn't know the story of Chanukah; didn't know there were dreidel games to play or special songs to sing. They didn't miss what they didn't know.

They placed in the bay window every year their silver coated plastic electric menorah with blue light bulbs. *Penny and I knew it was chintzy and ugly, a dime store menorah.* They kept their thoughts between themselves for the peewees' sake.

Dad said they were to twist the bulb on the middle "candle" every night of Chanukah, plus one additional candle each night for eight nights. They all agreed it looked nice to light one bulb from each side of the menorah every night, keeping it symmetrical. So that's how they did it, though Dad knew better.

Each child got a turn. Suzi wanted to go first. And as everyone knew that blue was her favorite color, no one minded.

Suzi twisted the tall, middle bulb. A blue light appeared. Oh, I wish, wish, wish for an Easy Bake Oven, Suzi thought. Then she turned the last bulb on the left. Another glorious burst of blue light shot into the room and reflected off the frosty window. In an instant, she changed her mind. Please let it be a special surprise, she prayed to the blue light.

Dad was still out of work and recovering from his stroke. But with financial help from Nannie, this Chanukah was a good one all around. Nannie knew what kind of year it had been. She understood they all needed something special.

And for once, everyone was happy. Sammy got a handsome brown leather suitcase for going away to college the next fall, and a shaving kit to match. Penny also got luggage for college – a fashionable light green suitcase and matching makeup case.

Glory's gift was a purple hued mini skirt in faux suede. *The very best gift ever.* Davey received a bright yellow dump truck with real moving parts. And Kit – she got the Easy Bake Oven, the one thing she'd wanted more than anything and had been praying for all along.

Suzi trembled as she ripped the snowflake patterned blue and white paper off her gift. She saw a large rectangular box. She closed her eyes and lifted the cover. Then she opened her eyes, took in her surprise, and gasped out loud.

She saw a beautiful doll, two feet tall with a ceramic face and peachy complexion. With large blue eyes that opened and closed, and curly golden brown hair. The doll wore a lovely royal blue gown with sparkly sleeves and a diamond tiara in her hair.

Suzi carefully took her doll out of its box and gave her the hug of a lifetime. That's when she noticed the silvery blue fairy wings.

She started to cry. "Hello, my old friend," she whispered. "How I've missed you, Blue Fairy."

The Blue Fairy winked back her silent hello. She had missed Suzi, too.

NANNIE AND SADIE

I should have stayed home. Why did I even come this year? Glory wondered as she sat watching Nannie knead the dough for the challah. Nannie was a good baker. Not as good as Ma, whose cinnamon bread, served warm with melting butter, filled the house with the scent of heaven.

Maybe it was in the forcefulness of Ma's kneading that the spirit of bread in its full Platonic sense was revealed. *Ma always said that slapping and pushing the dough around the breadboard was therapeutic. The idea is to get the dough as smooth and soft as a baby's bottom, she'd say.* Nannie's hands were old and weak compared with Ma's. But to give Nannie credit, her bread was good too.

Today, Nannie was silent as she lifted and pushed the dough with the palm of her hand, turned it, lifted and pushed again. Her eyes were angry but she wouldn't say a word. *Nannie can't be mad at me. After all, I've only been visiting a few days, and besides, she was already mad when I got here.*

It wasn't Glory's fault. It was just this - Nannie and Aunt Sadie weren't talking again. Their angry silences were more and more frequent. Glory didn't know why. This time, they hadn't spoken to each other since Chanukah, almost three months past.

Three months of deadly silence, and all because Sadie was furious at how much money her mother had spent on Joyce's family gifts. Sadie had railed at her mother. "You never spent that kind of money on me when I was a kid!" she exploded. "Here I am supporting you in your old age. I never have any privacy. I'm always coming home to a house filled with you. And now you're paying for gifts like those kids are royalty!"

Sadie couldn't stop. She had stored up anger for a lifetime. "I never got anything nice from you growing up. I was lucky to be let out of the corn bin for Chanukah, never mind get a fancy ceramic doll like some little princess, like Shirley Temple for Christ's sake. I would have killed for a doll like that! I got nothing, and now you're giving out presents like we're millionaires!"

Estelle had seen her Sadie angry many times before. She knew her daughter could be petty and selfish, jealous of Joyce who had six children and a husband who loved her.

Sadie had been married for only a short time to a man who adored her, who lavished her with gifts and handed over his military pension check to her every month. Sadie was tall with bright blonde hair and a movie star figure. She spent her paycheck on new dresses and manicures, and wore the latest fashions with great style. She could get any man she wanted. She was used to having them hanging all over her, used to fooling around and having fun.

Sadie was bored, so bored being married. She cheated on her new husband with another man. It was a cruel affair, only weeks after their wedding. The marriage ended without children. Despite the divorce, her ex-husband loved her, and the monthly pension checks kept coming.

"Be reasonable, Sadie," Estelle had responded. "You know that Herbie hasn't worked in months. The doctor said he may never be the same. They barely have enough to survive. And Davey, our little Davey, caught in that horrible fire."

Estelle started to break down. "Joyce has worked so hard, taking on extra shifts." She couldn't understand how her own daughter could be so uncaring. How did we come to this, she wondered as the tears filled her eyes.

"Joyce, Joyce! I'm so damn sick of hearing about how Joyce suffers, how hard her life is. What a bunch of crap!" Sadie continued her tirade. "Oh, what a good daughter Joyce is...Joyce is so smart...Joyce could have gone to college if we'd had the money...Joyce married Herb, the best man in town. Well, why the hell should I care about Joyce? What about me?" Sadie wouldn't stop. She was an adult having a child's tantrum.

Estelle thought fast. She made up a small lie, thinking it would help. "Jack sent most of the money. Most of it's from him. So you don't have to worry."

Sadie's anger filled the room right up to the ceiling. "That egotistic miser?" she demanded. "My rich and successful brother? He's never given a dime to me or to you, and don't you forget it! Since when did he start opening his fat cat wallet to Joyce?"

It was true that Jacob had all but abandoned his family. Jack was a kid from the slums; he didn't expect to attend college. It was something that his mother would never be able to afford. He hadn't given it much thought.

Joyce, though, had been desperately keen to go. But the tuition at Boston State was fifty dollars. It might have been a million; she never did get the chance. Though she wished for college more than anything, she was just a girl after all. Not destined for the academic or intellectual life. She married Herb instead.

Jack joined the Navy toward the end of the war. He shipped out but never saw any action. Afterwards, he came home to his Boston neighborhood and renewed old habits.

Joyce knew her under achieving brother Jacob only too well – she knew she'd have to keep him in line. She advised him that he'd be a fool not to take advantage of the G.I. Bill. *It was because of her insistence that Jack applied.* He was accepted to a college in the Midwest. He earned a degree in engineering and later worked his way through law school. He became a corporate attorney, a big shot for a major firm in Chicago.

Jack seldom visited home, and the fact was he didn't support his mother financially unless she or Joyce called with some real emergency. He considered his sister Sadie a self-centered spendthrift – loose with her money and herself, and nuts to boot. He wasn't about to send money that Sadie, no doubt, would squander.

If he did pay a bill for them, he'd pay it directly. Otherwise, he figured, Sadie would spend it on booze and a night out on the town. To put it gently, there was no love lost between the two of them.

Estelle was defeated. She realized she had said the wrong thing. There was no sense in stirring up a past that couldn't be corrected. "Sadie," she said sadly, "you're all I have. You've been good to me, a good daughter. I'd be all alone without you. My pension money, I'll keep tight in the bank from now on. Let's not fight."

Estelle meant it. Of her three children, only Sadie had taken her in, only Sadie had provided food for her to eat and a roof over her head all these years. So what if her daughter could be sharp and hateful? So what if she'd had too many men? Only God can judge. There's not a perfect one among us.

God forbid anything should happen to my Sadie, Estelle thought. I'm all alone, with only Sadie to buffer me from the cruel realities of old age. God willing, He'll take me soon, and Sadie can live her life.

But Sadie would have none of it. This is the last time I talk to that old hag, she thought. She can drop dead, for all I care.

That was last Chanukah. And now, on February school break, Aunt Sadie was in her bedroom with the door shut. She was playing solitaire and told Glory not to disturb her. She told Glory she'd be out for supper at five. She'd made it clear to Glory that she wasn't in the mood for company.

For crying out loud. This silent treatment stuff is the pits. Death toast burned to a crisp. It's worse than Mary, Queen of Scots, realizing she'll never be queen of England as well. Waiting for the axe to fall. Elizabeth had tried to talk sense into her, but no, she'd refused to listen, refused to give up her right to the throne.

Elizabeth hadn't a choice, because Mary was so damn pig headed and stubborn. Though to give Mary credit, she almost got her way. It was a close call, but truth be told, Elizabeth was always the superior. Talking it over couldn't have helped a thing. Off with her head — there was nothing left to say.

They were cousins who wouldn't speak. Women who should have been able to work things out; who might have been friends. Who might even have loved each other if they'd given it half a chance. Because in the end, there was nothing really to fight about — Elizabeth was the Virgin Queen, in whose honor savage lands were usurped, for whom all of Virginia in the New World was named. But Mary had a son, and a son trumps a virgin any time, any day. James would get the throne no matter what. The ending was clear. It was just a matter of time. God willing, of course.

"Nannie," said Glory in a no nonsense way. "There's nothing to do here until supper time. I want to take the bus into town. I could do some window shopping. I can go by myself. I have bus fare." Glory was sixteen years old. Downtown Boston was a ten minute ride. She'd been there a million times.

Estelle looked at Gloria, and through her misery saw not one, but two granddaughters. She saw the little girl, her beautiful tiny grandchild with the long curly dark hair and intense violet eyes. And she saw the grown girl, a magnet for trouble just like her Sadie. "No, my little Golda," she said. It was Glory's Hebrew name. "It's too dangerous for you to go alone into the city. There are street walkers. You might get mugged."

Glory bit her lip so hard she drew blood. She wanted to scream. *I need to hang out, to fool around, to have some fun. It's one thing to wait for reports from across the sea. Even a queen has to wait, sometimes for years, for news that could be oceans away.*

But queens are only women, after all, destined to wait and watch while knights in shining armor claim new lands in their names. While brothers run off to college and never return. While fathers go to war and come back broken men. While they themselves are left to keep a faith that never honestly included them in the first place. While sisters ponder their own brilliance without encouragement or support; while mothers watch disheartened as their daughters go astray. It was no wonder they couldn't speak. No wonder - there was nothing left for any of them to say.

And yet, beheading seems overly harsh. Better to let them work it out in their own way, in their own good time.

Meanwhile, the silence was deafening. Glory couldn't hold out much more, waiting for the new world she longed to see. *I am bored, so very bored.* And savages, all around and deep inside were stirring, moving to reclaim their lost land.

CAMILLE

"What do you think? Is it gorgeous, or what?" Glory turned around twice in front of the full length mirror in Camille's bedroom. She turned again and curtseyed to her friend. She raised her hand in a small wave as though she were a queen acknowledging her loyal subject.

Glory felt pretty. She was wearing a new jumper that she had just finished sewing. It was grey wool with a muted cream colored tweed pattern. She had a silky three quarter length sleeved blouse to go with it, a hand-me-down from her older cousin. She didn't love wearing hand-me-downs. And she certainly didn't love sewing her own clothes.

But there it is. The only way to get anything new or different to wear.

Glory and Penny, too, had resigned themselves long ago to this fact of their lives. They didn't think about it much anymore. Even Kit had started sewing to have something decent to wear.

Camille didn't answer. She looked at Glory and smiled just a little.

Rather full of herself at the moment, thinking of her matching grey tights and the cream colored barrette she had seen in the one clothing store their small downtown offered, Glory didn't wait for an answer. She continued on, as though she were talking to herself.

"Usually I like brighter colors, but this tweed really stood out in the fabric store. Don't you think it's pretty? It makes me feel English, or Scottish or something. You know, out for a stroll in the

Hundred Acre Wood with the horses and hounds, pip pip, cheerio old chap, shall we have ourselves a spot of tea?" She tossed her head and laughed.

I adore being British, pretending a rich and royal life.

Camille stared at Glory's dark hair. It was pulled straight back off her face in a rather severe fashion, and piled high on the back of her head with long curly strands hanging down asymmetrically. Most girls would need a softer look to enhance their features, a teased up or bouffant affair with satin ribbons, but Glory had the most intense violet eyes and striking complexion. She could wear her hair anyway she wanted and still look good.

A little too good, Camille thought. It keeps her from knowing her place.

"Help me measure the hem, will you? Glory asked. "I want it as short as they'll let me wear it." Glory laughed again. Her miniskirts were her freedom, her unusual hairstyles a refuge from the stultifying conformity of the day in their old cow town.

Camille held pins in her teeth while Glory stood on a chair and turned around little by little. She silently placed a pin every inch or so all the way around the jumper to set the hem.

Camille couldn't talk holding pins with her teeth anyway, but she wasn't in the mood to chat. She was thinking about Glory, how Glory had been her best friend for two years. They had met the first day of high school in French class.

Camille had seen Gloria around the halls in middle school, but hadn't been in a class with her before. She'd heard the eighth grade gossip about her. How Glory was brilliant, one of those super smart kids who knows all the answers without having to try.

She remembered back in fifth grade, how Glory was so good in math, she had been chosen to demonstrate the new math curriculum to the faculty at the local teaching college. Glory and her friend Beth, and a few other math freaks had sat in front of a whole auditorium of educators. The professor had posed problems to the panel of kids, requiring they use the new math skills they had learned only at the beginning of the presentation. No rote memorization, only logic and deconstruction of formulas could be used. It was meant to be challenging and fun. The audience had clapped and cheered for these young children who picked up so quickly on the new way of thinking about math. And for themselves, for designing it in the first place.

Camille only remembered this because a photo of Glory and a story had been reported in the local newspaper. Camille's mother was a teacher and had read all about the new math. She'd asked Camille if she knew this girl in the news, and had said "You should be friends with her. She looks nice and obviously smart. You could learn a thing or two from this girl." Camille of course didn't take her mother's advice. She was good enough in school, thank you, and didn't feel the need to be a genius.

She'd heard that Glory wasn't just smart but really weird too. They said she made up fairy tales in her head and pretended to be a princess - cute when you're eight but not at fifteen.

The popular crowd would have nothing to do with her. It wasn't enough to be pretty and slim to be a member of the popular crowd. You had to dumb down if you were smart and a girl. You had to have money for nice clothes. You had to conform to the popular crowd's rules, which meant turning mean and petty, sarcastic and demeaning. You could be nice underneath or on the rare occasions when you were one on one. But not on the surface or when you're with the crowd. You couldn't stand out from the crowd in any meaningful way.

Camille herself hadn't been ready for the popular crowd. She was the prettiest of them all and willing to conform to their narrow dress code. But she didn't want to be really mean, and she, sort of, liked people who were different, as long as they weren't too different. She decided not to try it out. Because being dumped from the popular crowd would have been a worse fate than never making it in the first place.

[Other reports about Glory through Camille's eighth grade grapevine: Patty]

Patty adored the Beatles, a passion she and Glory shared. Patty told Camille that Glory was really interesting but it was true that she was stuck in her own strange world. "She's odd," Patty had said, "but fun to be around. And she's got so much energy, always dancing, always making dumb jokes, goofy stuff. Of course we both love Paul the best. He's so dreamy." Patty's mother called Glory a "hot ticket." It was the highest of compliments - she liked Gloria a lot. Gloria was never dull.

[Other reports about Glory through Camille's eighth grade grapevine: Rosemarie]

Rosemarie had been a good friend to Glory all through middle school. Their best friend status had diminished over time and was now dead, but not for any special reason. She felt a little jealous that Camille showed interest in her former best friend. But truth be told, Glory was in all the honors classes and Rosemarie in the standard. They never saw each other in school. They forgot what they had in common. They simply went their separate ways but kept good memories of each other.

[Other reports about Glory through Camille's eighth grade grapevine: Beth]

Beth defended Glory down the line. You couldn't say anything bad about Gloria with Beth around. That was because when Beth moved from the city to their town in first grade, she was so smart they had to double promote her into Gloria's class. Beth was a whole year younger than everyone else and a tiny girl to start. The school janitor, Hank, had to cut her desk legs down so she could reach the desk top to write. She and Glory clicked immediately and became best friends.

One day a month or so after Beth first arrived in town, a skinny crew cut boy named Bobby was teasing Beth out in the playground. "You're so ugly! Skinny and ugly! You got cooties, cooties in your hair!" he exclaimed loudly to anyone who would listen. "Beth's got cooties in her hair, Beth's got cooties in her hair!" he chanted nastily. Several of Bobby's friends began to laugh. Beth started to cry.

Gloria was outraged. Why would anyone pick on her sweet friend Beth? "She does not have cooties – she has pretty hair!" Gloria countered. Her eyes were flashing, her head held high like a monarch defending the royal crown against the mob.

"And you're a stupid jerk, Bobby! How old are you anyway – eight? Still in second grade and I bet you can't even add two plus two! Still reading *Dick and Jane*! You're the ugliest boy I ever met, for sure!"

Glory put her arm around Beth and trounced off. They sat on the swings and swung as high as the swings would allow. It was their freedom; their escape from mean spirited remarks and idiotic comments, from hurt feelings and wounds deeply cut. A time to process what they'd heard, to discard anything that didn't make sense.

"What are cooties?" Glory asked her mother later. "Bobby said Beth has cooties in her hair. It made Beth cry."

Joyce sighed. Why is the world so damn cruel? she wondered. Beth's all of six years old. Can't they just leave her be?

"Cooties are another word for lice," Ma explained to her innocent young daughter. "They're bugs that can get stuck in your hair if you are dirty and don't wash. They itch and you need special shampoo to get rid of them."

Ma continued. "But I know Beth doesn't have lice. She's a clean child. Beautiful. Bobby said that because she's black. He must have heard it from his parents, because I know he couldn't have made that up on his own. There are many people who hate anyone with black skin or brown skin, or any color skin but white. They will say and do all kinds of bad things to people who have black skin. It's terribly unnecessary and cruel - attitudes left over from the days when blacks were slaves. It's one of the great sorrows of our country."

Glory was proud to have parents who weren't hateful to people just because they were black. She didn't know what slaves were, but it sounded very bad. When she became queen, she would never have slaves in her country, she was very sure.

She felt happy to have a mother who said Beth was a beautiful child. Because Glory knew that Beth was smart, smarter than she'd ever be. Beth lived in a clean house, much cleaner than her own. And she was sweet and pretty and wore nice clothes. There was nothing bad that anyone could say about Beth that could be true in any way. Anyone who said bad things - well, now at the tender age of seven, Glory knew just how ugly people could be. And it had nothing to do with the color of their skin. It came straight from inside.

[Camille's first decision - ninth grade]

Of course, much time had passed since Beth first moved to town. In eighth grade, Camille quizzed everyone she knew about Gloria the Smart and Weird. In the first week of high school, she decided to take a chance and try her out as a friend. It was a match for the ages. It seemed that only minutes passed before their status changed to best friends forever.

~~~~~~

Camille stared at Glory as she turned round on the chair. Why is she looking so self-satisfied today? It's not like that jumper is a prom gown or anything, she thought. And the seams aren't straight at the zipper. Glory sews a lot but she isn't good at it. Actually, I think the jumper's kind of ugly. Not her color at all.

Glory's colors were purple, blue and gold - garish and too bold in Camille's eyes. Camille preferred petal pink. Petal pink was classy and understated, and brought out the best in Camille's blue eyes and blond hair. Petal pink against her creamy white skin made her look almost Scandinavian, maybe Norwegian, a beautiful ice princess. She felt like a fairy princess in petal pink, or a beautiful ballerina. The difference is, Camille decided - unlike Glory, I know I'm not a princess or a ballerina. I live in the real world.

And her hair — nobody wore their hair like Glory. It wasn't how anyone at school would think to do it. Camille couldn't wear her hair that way, straight back and up. Not that it would look bad, of course it wouldn't. It's just that it wouldn't look great. Her own hair was fine and straight and would never stay up in a bun or twist. It would fall out in minutes. Plus she'd just cut a few bangs, too short to stay back in an elastic. It just wouldn't work, and besides, who but Glory would want it that way?

Camille was sick of Glory presuming she was so much smarter. Even though Glory didn't come right out and say it, Camille knew she thought it. Camille was no slouch. She was better at French and just as good at science. In the real world, where it counted, Camille knew she was better. It's not like anyone actually uses calculus in the real world, she believed.

And what was that curtsey business? And the waving of the

hand, like Camille was some peasant only there for the purpose of taking up hems? She was no seamstress, and no servant of Gloria's, that was for sure.

She was tired of Gloria's queen act, bored to death with it actually. Her friend was odd and totally strange. It had never bothered her before. But now the whole business was getting old fast. Two years of Maid Marion and Mary Queen of Scots, the great Elizabeth and Camelot. When was Glory going to grow up? When would she stop living her fairy tale existence?

[Mike]

Camille was seeing Mike more and more. It had been over a half year since they first started dating, eight and a half months to be precise. At first it had been quite casual, but now they were a real item.

Mike's the best boyfriend I'm ever likely to have, she thought. Older by a year, he was the finest looking boy in school – wicked handsome. And he was reasonably smart, college bound and drove a Mustang, which was almost as good as a Porsche.

He dressed like an early Beatle before they went all hippy, with slightly shaggy but carefully groomed hair and fashionable clothes. He played it cool, never overdressing, and knew how to please Camille's parents by wearing the occasional button down shirt and khaki pants. Not too preppy, not hippy – just right.

Camille hadn't told Glory, but things were getting hot and heavy between her and her boyfriend. Mike was seventeen and an upperclassman. He expected Camille to understand that an older man has needs.

She was scared at first and not ready. They started with kissing and moved quickly to petting. Mike still wasn't satisfied. He told

Camille he could get another girlfriend anytime. He loved her, but how long could she expect him to wait? He had his needs, after all, and the whole world was changing, wasn't it? Didn't everyone talk about free love? The signs were everywhere —free love, make love not war, love is all you need, peace and love, all you need is love, love-love-love. Everyone said so. It was a new era. What was her problem?

[Camille's problem]

Camille's problem was not that she wasn't ready, though she truly wasn't. It was not that she couldn't read the signs. The signs were everywhere — you couldn't miss them. And it was not that she didn't love Mike.

Camille's problem was with her best friend Glory. Because Mike had become insanely jealous of her. Of how inseparable Camille and Glory were, of how much Camille enjoyed Glory's company, of what great friends they had grown to be. Of how crazy it was that his girlfriend liked Glory more than himself.

He wondered if that made Camille a lezzie, because everyone knew that Glory was one. His friend Billy had taken her for a walk through the field to test it out the summer before. They had made a bet with a few of their friends. Billy was a good looking boy. No normal girl would turn him away. It was a simple formula, an easy test.

Billy had reported back — for sure, Gloria was a lezzie. Mike had lost ten bucks on that one. He had risked his reputation with the popular crowd to date Camille, lesbian loving Camille.

But now he had had enough. It was Gloria or him — Camille had to choose. She had to go all the way with him. She had to give up seeing Glory, or it was all over between them. Mike had given Camille the ultimatum, and he wasn't joking.

[Camille's second decision - tenth grade]

Camille looked at Glory's cream colored blouse. She noticed a small tear at the seam under the arm. Usually if she saw a flaw in Glory's clothing, she'd point it out so she could fix it. It was the nice thing to do. Camille didn't have to wear hand-me-downs and old clothing. She wasn't rich but she wasn't poor either. Her family had enough for her to buy new clothes every season.

Camille said nothing about the tear. She looked down and saw that Glory's slipper shoes were scuffed and old. One knee sock had fallen down. It was old, the elastic stretched. Camille hadn't seen, really seen before now how used Glory's clothes could look. How worn and decrepit. How unfashionable. Not hip and cool like she tried to pretend, but old. Ancient, really. Almost ugly.

As Camille put the last pin into Glory's hem, she saw something else. She didn't know what it was at first. Maybe it was a hanging thread. Then she looked closer and gasped. It was a scar, two or three inches long, running down the side of Gloria's thigh. Next to it, there was a second scar. And a third and a fourth.

Glory pulled the jumper off over her head, being careful not to dislodge the pins. As she did, Camille looked intently at her friend. On the other thigh she saw four more scars, all the same. All jagged, ugly, horrible, deforming, defacing scars. They were the most terrifying sights Camille had ever seen. She jumped up and ran to the toilet in the bathroom down the hall. She vomited out her guts, the vomit of a lifetime.

When she came back to her bedroom, Glory had pulled on a pair of dungarees and an old sweatshirt. She'd left her boots and coat by the back door. It was mud season and chilly weather, and a two mile walk home.

"Thanks for helping me pin up my jumper," Glory said to Camille as she walked out. "See you tomorrow in class."

Camille didn't answer. She looked at Glory's coat. It was a threadbare man's coat, several sizes too big for Glory's small frame. On her head was a knit cap with a pull in the back, and around her neck, an ugly rust colored scarf. Who *are* you? Camille thought. You're not the girl I believed I knew.

Glory walked down the sidewalk toward home. *Why was Camille so quiet? It isn't like her to be silent and unfriendly. Though, since Mike became her steady date, Camille had changed. Maybe she's sick. I thought I heard her throw up in the bathroom. I hope she's okay.* Glory worried about her best friend all the way home.

~~~~~~

"Bonjour, mes amis. J'espère vous avez eu un bon weekend. Gloria, s'il vous plaît, make up a sentence with passé composé of the verb 'to descend.'" Mme. Picard stood expectantly, knowing Gloria would get it right.

She's turned over a new leaf this year, never missing a Monday morning. She's a real leader, Mme. Picard thought. Good for getting the class off to a correct start at this hellish hour. Mme. Picard hated mornings as much as Glory, but couldn't let it show.

"J'ai descendue les escaliers," Gloria replied.

Hmmm, thought Mme. Picard. I wonder what's wrong with Glory today? "Not quite," she said aloud to the class. "Anyone else?"

Camille raised her hand. "Je suis descendue les escaliers." She didn't need Mme. Picard to tell her she was correct. Camille was the reigning princess of French II.

Glory looked back at Camille and smiled. She had been worried that Camille was sick, and was happy to see her well and in class. *There's something wrong with Camille. Something deeply wrong, a big change of some kind. A secret that she hadn't told me. Why, I don't know. Camille didn't even said hi to me this morning.*

Camille's so good at French. Maybe in a past life, she was a great French queen. Eleanor of Aquitaine perhaps, because of course Camille speaks English as well, and Eleanor was queen of both France and England, and mother of Richard the Lionheart of Crusades fame. If Maid Marion weren't just a legend, she might have been presented to Eleanor in her royal court after King Richard came back from abroad and pardoned Robin Hood.

Of course, Marion and Robin aren't real. It's idiotic to mix history with fairy tales. And besides, Camille is too modern and fashionable to be a medieval queen. More likely, a descendant of some later age, perhaps the Renaissance or Reformation. Maybe she's Marie Antoinette reincarnate.

Hmmm, I don't like the idea of Camille as Marie Antoinette. It was a disturbing thought. My best friend isn't arrogant, isn't dismissive. Self-centered but not to the point of cruelty. Yes, she is a great beauty just like the French queen, but that's where the comparison ends. Camille could never starve those around her while she herself lives in luxury. She could never be hateful or unkind to the dirty, unwashed masses. I know Camille better than that.

Camille looked at Glory sitting at the front of the class. She watched as Glory turned around to give Camille a smile.

Camille saw that Glory was wearing a faded navy blue corduroy jumper with a lavender turtle neck. You could see the faded line around the bottom where the jumper hem had been taken down. She must have made that in eighth grade, Camille thought. She'd seen her wear that same outfit at least a hundred times.

Worse, Glory wore a purple beaded headband around her forehead. She looks like a cross between a hippy freak and Ivanhoe, Camille thought. What did I ever see in her? She's making this so easy.

Camille re-read the note she had carefully composed in her

bedroom the night before. She'd spent an hour on it. Yes, she thought, this is good enough. She folded the note into a compact square and wrote *Glory* on the top.

She tapped the shoulder of the boy sitting in front of her. "Pass this to Gloria," she whispered. The note made its way up to the top of the class where Glory sat.

Glory took the note. *Aha!* She recognized the handwriting. *Maybe this is the great secret.* She opened the note in the shelter of her French textbook, hiding it from Mme. Picard's eyes. She read the words. It was indeed a message from Camille, the reigning princess of French II.

"*Gloria,*" the note read. "*Our friendship is over. I used to think you were cool but actually your clothes are ugly. And by the way, no one wears their hair like that. I love Mike and we're together. Mike hates your guts and so do his friends, and now I know why. I knew you were strange but I had no idea until yesterday how psychotic you really are. I don't want to talk to you ever again. Don't even try, Camille.*"

Gloria sat in shock, frozen in her seat. It was as though her heart had stopped beating. She couldn't think of what happened yesterday that made Camille hate her today. *Was it the tweed?* She couldn't move. She couldn't think. And then with a jerk, she forced her body up out of the chair. She grabbed her books and ran out of the classroom. "Excusez-moi, excusez-moi, pardon," she cried to Mme. Picard as she bolted out the door.

Qu'est ce qui se passe? Mme. Picard worried. It was not like her best student to be sick. Something must be wrong, really wrong.

Camille watched Glory run from the truth. She felt a small pang of regret, just a little one, that the end of their friendship had come so abruptly, with so little warning.

But there was nothing to be done about it. Camille had decided.

She was going all the way with Mike, the love of her life. She would be one of the popular crowd, someone all the ugly people in school would wish they could be.

Next year, she'd be prom queen for sure. She could already picture her gown. It would be strapless - petal pink flowing silk in multiple layers. Her beautiful blonde hair would be swept up with diamond barrettes and pink tulle. Her blue eyes would shine, her complexion glowing like pearls. Like an ice princess from the north. Camille smiled just thinking of the sight.

~~~~~~

Glory ran out the double doors by the bus entrance and down the street, through the mud, almost a mile to the field across from her home. She found the swings and flung herself with her muddy shoes onto the nearest one. She swung and swung with all her might while her face turned pink and her ears red with cold, her books dumped into the snow.

They could give her detention if they wanted. They could expel her for all she cared. Her world was gone. The best friend she'd ever had in her entire life was gone. Camille the Beautiful had turned ugly, and it had come straight from inside.

It was another lesson to be processed and only discarded if found untrue, a null and empty hypothesis. The bond between a woman and her man is stronger, more compelling than any friendship. There is an undeniable logic to the formula, a construct that can't be further reduced. A prime, with no derivatives.

Glory played the maiden queen, not the court jester. She was no fool. Think of Marion and Robin. Even a virgin could see that.

~~~~~~

Postscript: Mike was right about one thing — it was a new era. Whenever the spirit moved her, Glory kept on wearing her hair pulled straight, up and in a knot on the back of her head in asymmetrical patterns. Sometimes she added an Indian headband. Within a short time, other girls around school, those with a pretty face and the right kind of hair, those who could carry it off, copied Gloria's new look. Glory, they said, is unique and original. A real trend setter. I want to look just like her, the hip and cool girls said. Forget those plastic, old fashioned beauty queens - Glory's got real style. A style all her own.

Glory took some small comfort in their flattery.

THE PROM

Spring had come again, a time of great confusion in the natural world of southeastern Massachusetts. A time for tiny delicate crocus to bud, only to be buried and sometimes crushed under a late snowfall. For robins to fly home from their wanderings even before the earthworms work their way out of the frozen ground.

Azaleas bloom one week; daffodils another. Antisocial forsythia's already come and gone along with the snowdrops. Cherry blossoms and rhododendrons and tulips awake in no particular order. Crab apples usually flower last, but not always.

Skunk and raccoon, squirrel and chipmunk scurry out of their nests willy-nilly, looking for something fresh to eat after the long lonely winter. Everybody's lean and hungry. All living things in the spring look for their chance, search for a place to thrive, jockey for position.

Perhaps there is harmony and concordance in a New York spring, or in Pennsylvania, or Washington DC. But in southeastern Massachusetts, Mother Nature cries out a dissonant prelude. She doesn't desire a symphony of bloom. She fights to keep everyone and everything under her domain on guard.

She prefers to conduct a guessing game. Can I keep that blue jay from stealing my nest? wonders the worried female cardinal just laying her eggs. Maybe I could use that nest to lay my eggs, the tired female blue jay thinks, searching for a suitable place to land. It is survival of the fittest, and Mother Nature is cruel. She's tough, demanding disorderly progressions in spring. Because she knows once summer comes, both flora and fauna - anyone who's survived the spring grows strong.

There is an inevitable harmony in the summer solstice. That's the easy part. But it's the getting there that counts. Spring brings chaos and uncertainty, discordant notes and solo acts whose timing may be all off. It's meant to make us fit and able. Any good mother wants her children fit and able for the times to come. It's the law of nature.

~~~~~~

The peewees were fighting again. "There's something about the end of the school year," said Ma, "that has everyone riled up. Everyone wants out. No one can wait - for summer to come, to grow up just a little, to be counted as a third grader instead of a second; an adult in high school instead of a child still in middle. Nothing is ever good enough for now. You're all the same, all impatient, all cut from the same cloth." Ma understood the feeling, but still, the kids were annoying her no end.

Suzi wouldn't stop whining. She simply couldn't get along. She counted the days and hours for two events to occur. First, the day she turned ten, with two digits instead of one in her age – no small thing, two digits meant you weren't a mere child anymore, but on your way to teenager. And second, to finish with elementary forever and be a big kid in middle school. Even though that wouldn't happen until fall and it was only May and she still had four weeks of fourth grade left.

She picked on Davey until he was ready to sock her. "Red Rover, Red Rover, send baby Davey over!" Suzi chanted mercilessly. Davey was now seven and growing noticeably day by day. Like a baby bird, he'd soon be full grown, or at least grown enough to hold his own against Suzi.

She'd better watch out, Davey thought. Hitting was forbidden in their house. Ma wouldn't allow it, but alternatives popped up daily during the spring. One of these days I'll shove her face into her plate of spaghetti if she doesn't stop teasing me. Davey imagined the scene with great satisfaction.

Davey had a secret place up in the second attic, the one way at the top of their old farm house. He'd sneak up two flights with a black crayon and draw on the smooth parts of the crumbling slat walls.

He was a talented and accomplished artist. He drew light bulbs and flights of stairs, mazes and pictures of rats and mice and bats; and spooky Halloween subjects like skeletons and skulls. You needed a flashlight to see Davey's "cave" drawings, an old musty closet in which he had drawn cars and dump trucks, and volcanoes with flames shooting out of them like fireworks.

His best drawing was of Suzi with her head in a noose, hanging from a rafter. Her eyes popped out of their sockets and her tongue hung down and dripped spit. Above it he had written *My stupid sister Suzi*. To give Davey credit, the drawing revealed ability beyond his years. He'd shown it to Sammy who hooted up a storm of laughter.

The attic was a refuge for Davey; the drawings a needed outlet for his frustrations. After all, it wasn't easy being youngest, constantly being treated as though he were still a baby. Ready for a big leap into something new but having to wait, to take orders from everyone including his whiny sister Suz.

Davey felt separate from the rest of his family, even from Sammy who, though years older, enjoyed having a brother after all those sisters. His siblings were always coming and going, most of the time without him. No one wanted to play cops and robbers with him anymore, or cowboys and Indians. No one took him seriously or asked his opinion. He'd wanted to build a fort in the scrub pines at the edge of their yard – none of them offered to help.

Kit used to be nice to me, he thought. She used to hide in the red and gold leaves with me. That was fun. She liked to play hide and seek, and took me sledding too. And she always shared her ice creams if I asked.

But now that Kit was eleven and a grown up middle school-er, she had stopped playing with Davey. She considered herself too old to consort with a little baby brother. She was acting uppity and cared more about clothes and how she looked and friends than having fun with him.

Lately, any time Davey asked, Kit would turn him down. Did she want to play catch? No. Would she balance on the seesaw with him, or slide down the slide? No and no. Did she want to play king of the mountain, or even climb a tree? The answer was always the same. Kit's growing up was sad for Davey. He wasn't on the same track. He couldn't keep up.

One day during that unruly spring, Penny came flying home from school with an enormous smile on her face. She ran down the street and flung herself into the house.

She dumped her books and immediately found a round aluminum pan, one of a pair that Kit used to bake cakes and she used for fudge. Penny loved making fudge, a dark, chocolate fudge to which, on occasion, she added walnuts. It was her way of connecting with the mother inside her, the nurturer she one day would be.

Fudge was her celebration, almost like praying except that you could eat the results. Prayer for the body, not the soul. She enjoyed cooking it more than eating it; though it went without saying, they were all quite partial to her sweet concoctions.

She cut a pat of unsalted butter and smeared it over the pan so the fudge wouldn't stick. She got out the pot for melting rock hard squares of Baker's bitter chocolate. She'd make a mixture of the chocolate, milk, a little vanilla extract, and more butter. To it, she'd add a sugar syrup that tested at just the right consistency, the soft ball stage.

Penny was like a chemist carefully weighing her potions and medicines, looking for exactly the right temperature and viscosity. When she found it, everything would come together and into the buttered pan, then cooled until hardened. Honestly, there wasn't a better dessert in the world than Penny's homemade fudge.

Davey saw Penny making the fudge. "Penny!" he implored. "I want to help – can I help?" He was bored and had nothing to do. It was Glory's turn to babysit after school. She was working on a paper for English class and ignoring him entirely.

Penny hadn't known that anyone else was home. She brushed past Davey and ran into the dining room where Glory's books were all spread out. "I didn't know you were here!" Penny gushed. "You won't believe what happened! When I tell you what happened, you just won't believe it!"

Glory looked at Penny. Her eyes were glowing and she looked happier than Glory had ever seen her before.

Penny will be graduating from high school in only a few weeks. She'll be an adult, all grown up, and off on her way to college in the fall. Penny had been accepted to the University of Massachusetts in Amherst, way out in the western part of the state. It was a three hour drive or more.

She'll be going away and not coming home until Thanksgiving. I already know all about that, that can't be what's getting Penny so excited. What could top getting accepted to college and actually escaping this old cow town? I can't think of anything better.

"I'm going to the prom! I'm going to the prom!" Penny shrieked. She could barely keep her words apart, she was so crazed. "Steve B____ asked me today. Steve's sister Gina told Naomi, and of course Naomi told me, last week he was thinking of asking me, but

I didn't believe her." Naomi was Penny's best friend.

"He's so shy, I never thought he'd ask. Don't you think he's kind of cute? Oh my God, I can't believe it, I can't believe it!" Penny danced around the room, and ran back to check her fudge. She had never expected to attend the prom. That was for slim, pretty girls with nice clothes and manicured nails, not for girls like Penny and Naomi who had a few pounds to lose and didn't know the first thing about flirting with a boy.

Sammy came through the back door just then. He was also headed to college in the fall. Sammy was always a brilliant student, right at the top of his class. He had received a full scholarship to an Ivy League college. He'd topped Penny once again, as he had done his whole life. It seemed that right out of the womb, Sammy was the superior twin.

He'd asked the divine Denise to the prom, the girl of his dreams who wore tight sweaters to great effect. She'd answered yes, though she'd secretly hoped for a taller date. She'd have to wear flats. Sammy wasn't tall and never would be. That didn't stop his already oversized ego from inflating. He couldn't be any more full of himself.

"What's all the fuss?" Sammy asked as he poked at the fudge. It was still soupy — wouldn't be ready until after supper. He looked in the bread box and scooped out some saltines.

"Not that it's any of your business," Penny answered huffily, "but I've just been asked to the prom." She tried hard to hide her smile. Her freckled face was pink with delight.

Sammy didn't look up. He didn't miss a beat. "Big deal. Who's the jerk who's so desperate, he'd ask *you* out? Not that I care."

Penny's face fell. Sammy had, like a balloon filled with too much hot air, popped all the joy out of her exciting news.

"You're so ugly," Sammy calmly continued, "it's a wonder any boy in school would ask you. The guy must be from the loony bin for the criminally insane!"

Sammy knew just what to say to get his sister's goat. It was so easy, it wasn't fun anymore. He didn't even think Penny was all so ugly like she used to be. She'd kind of matured and didn't look all that bad. It was just his tradition, his way of making it clear who was still in charge, which twin ruled.

"Sammy, you're so mean. I hate you – I hate you!" Penny started to cry. She ran through the living room, up the front staircase, and up to her room.

Sammy called after her. "Who'd want to date a porker like you? I'll bet they don't make a dress big enough or ugly enough to fit you!" Sammy got out the peanut butter and jelly. He made a stack of crackers and poured himself some milk.

Davey saw his chance. "Sammy, want to play catch?" he asked expectantly.

Sammy was about to say no when he saw the look in his little brother's eyes. "Sure, you grossly overweight smelly twerp," he said fondly. "Just as soon as I finish up here."

Glory heard Sammy and hoped that the finish would come soon. She couldn't wait for college to begin. With most twins, everything comes in twos, measure by measure, melody up tempo, harmony in sync.

But in the case of Sammy and Penny, they were a pair always out of tune. Yes, there were two of everything, but in diametric opposition. One was bitter and the other sweet. One was joyful, the other cruel. One strong, the other weak. Tenor, contralto. Piano, forte. But it wasn't just the twins. They were all falling flat, every one of them off their beat. The cacophony was real.

The peewees will miss Sammy.

Yet she would pray to Persephone herself, goddess of new beginnings, for college to come. But here was the rub, why that prayer would prove a dissonant chord. The finish that got rid of Sammy meant losing dear Penny too. There was no winning, no resolution to an unhappy, discordant score.

~~~~~~

Penny pulled the full length slip over her head and slid it down into place. She pressed her feet into new satin pumps, dyed spring green to match her prom gown. She looked at herself in the mirror at the dressing table in the bedroom she shared with Glory.

Just for tonight, she thought, I'll be Queen Penny as Glory had once proclaimed me to be. Not "the Good" though. I'll be Queen Penny the Lovely, just for one night. For the very first time, Penny believed in herself, believed it could be true. "Glory, would you help me step into my dress?"

Gloria took Penny's spring green gown off the hanger and brought it to her. It was gorgeous. Penny had worked every day after school and two entire weekends on this dress. She and Ma and Glory had picked out the shiny satin fabric and matched up a zipper and thread, tiny rosettes, and yards of ribbon.

Then they'd driven to the dress shop two towns over. Penny had ordered satin shoes to be dyed to match. Ma bought her long white gloves with tiny white covered buttons, and an evening purse, silky white with sequins. It was the splurge of a lifetime.

Penny stepped into her dress and Glory zipped up the back. It was a simple gown, a sleeveless A-line with an empire waist and square neck. The ribbon held at the waist and tied in a bow in the back, with long ends hanging down. Penny had made a bow for her hair out of the same satiny ribbon. Her hair was pulled back in an elegant twist with lots of bobby pins and hair spray, the bow placed carefully in the back. Ma had loaned her a pearl necklace - not real pearls, because of course Ma had none, but they looked real enough.

She didn't often wear makeup, but tonight she had borrowed Glory's midnight blue mascara and eye liner. She had rouged her cheeks and painted her lips with a soft pink lipstick that matched her nail color.

It couldn't be denied – Penny looked exquisite, the finest she'd ever looked in her life. Glory and Ma, Kit and Suzi all said so. Even Davey looked smitten, though they chased him out of the room for being a boy.

And for once, Glory was the handmaiden, not the queen. *It was a new experience, being ruled, no longer the ruler. A different feeling that I enjoyed more than I thought I would. It was Penny's moment, not mine. I gave up my reign to Penny's domain. I wouldn't do it for anyone else except Penny. Because Penny is the Good, and tonight, the Lovely. She deserves happiness. Penny deserves to lay claim to the best that life can offer. There isn't any other person on earth that I can say that about.*

There was a knock on the door, and Davey let Steve B___ into the house. He was carrying a corsage with white and pink roses to pin on Penny's dress.

Oh no, thought Gloria, as she raced down the stairs to greet him. He'll see the disaster we live in. Why did Davey do something stupid like that? None of us let even our best friends into the house. It's always a mess, more than a mess. It's downright filthy.

Nobody ever cleans unless important company is coming. Then it will be a flurry of activity, throwing things into closets and closing the doors, last minute sweeps with the broom to get peas and other shrunken, misshapen vegetables out from under the table, dumping full ashtrays into the trash. Our house is dirty – no place to bring a prom date, that's for certain.

Gloria thought quickly as Steve began to look around the living room, his eyes widening in surprise at the peeling wallpaper and smoky mess he took in. "Hi Steve," she said in a falsely cheery voice. "I'm Glory, Penny's sister. Penny's not quite ready yet. It's such a nice night – why don't we wait outside for a while? She'll be with you soon enough."

She took Steve's arm and guided him back out the door. As they left, Glory looked back at Davey and gave him an angry scowl. Davey was just starting to grow up. He didn't know what he had done wrong, couldn't know how important pretense and pride can be to a teenage girl.

They walked out the door. Steve couldn't believe his luck. He had been hoping to catch sight of the gorgeous Gloria, only a sophomore but already the talk of the boys' locker room.

The guys said all kinds of disgusting things about all the girls, but when talk turned to Glory, they really went to all out. They said she hitchhiked everywhere and put out along the way. That you could take her under the bleachers and she'd lift up her shirt and show you what she's got. That she was a lezzie but it didn't stop her from screwing every boy she met. Steve didn't really believe all these stories, but he was a red blooded male, and he could hope they were true, couldn't he?

Gloria walked out with Steve to his car. She was marking time. "Those are beautiful flowers," she commented. "They match Penny's dress really well. She's going to love them. Penny's so excited about the prom. Aren't you too?"

Steve was more excited to be standing next to Gloria. He thought, this is my only chance. Better take it.

She was saying, "The theme is Spring Time in Paris. I saw the gym. Your class did such a great job with the decorations. I wish I were going. Oh well, maybe next year."

Steve was thinking, next year is too late. I have to make my move now.

He grabbed the back of Glory's neck. He pulled her toward him and roughly kissed her.

Gloria was utterly shocked. She turned her head and fought to push away. Steve dropped Penny's corsage to the ground. A tiny white rose broke off and tumbled to the street. He pawed at Glory's shirt with his free hand. He tried to kiss her again.

Penny was leaving the house, walking out through the door to meet Steve, her prom date. She'd never been so excited; never felt so good about herself or about how she looked. She was thinking, Spring Time in Paris is the most fabulous theme ever, and Steve is the best date I'll ever have.

Then she looked over to Steve's car and let out a small cry. There was her prom date, her king consort, making out with Gloria.

Steve looked up and saw Penny. He pushed Glory aside. He picked up the fallen corsage and walked over to her. "Honest, Penny," he said. "I was just standing there waiting for you when your sister came along. She's weird, I guess we all know that. But you...you sure look beautiful tonight. May I have the honor of pinning on your corsage?"

Penny had a choice to make. She could cry and ruin her midnight blue mascara. She could run back upstairs, tear off her dress, and miss the prom entirely. The best night of her life, all ruined on account of Gloria. Or, she could accept Steve's explanation, block out the pain, and go on to the prom. Where she'd be Queen Penny the Lovely, at least for one night.

She made her choice. Really, the only thing to do. She let Steve pin on the broken corsage. She let him open the car door while she settled herself in. She let Steve close the door and drive her to the prom. They had a wonderful time. The dance of a lifetime. A treasured memory of high school days, never to be repeated.

When she got home, it was late, two a.m. or so. On the way, Penny had let Steve kiss her and feel her up. It seemed the thing to do, the time honored tradition and activity on the post prom calendar of events. Penny needed to grow up sometime. She might as well have started with Steve.

Glory couldn't sleep. *I waited up for Penny. I needed to explain. I knew that what happened must have looked bad, really bad, but it wasn't my fault. I didn't do anything wrong. Really, there is a good explanation for everything.* "Penny," Gloria begged, "you won't believe what happened."

But Penny would have none of it. She couldn't talk to Glory, not even when the calming strength of summer solstice arrived. She wouldn't speak.

Maybe it was because for once Penny ruled, and not her gifted sister. Penny got a taste of being queen. Being queen, even for a day, was better than eating a whole pan full of homemade fudge. Being queen was manna from heaven. Penny relished the role and would not relinquish her throne. She'd found her power; she wouldn't let it go.

That could have been it, a perfectly reasonable motivation. A logical assertion no one could deny.

Or maybe it was the spring. The cruel, heartless, difficult, demanding, dissonant song of spring that was to blame.

~~~~~~

Postscript: Suzi turned ten on the longest day of the year. She now had two digits in her age and was that much closer to becoming preteen and a grown up middle school-er. To celebrate, Kit, who had practiced on her Easy Bake Oven and was turning into an accomplished dessert maker, baked a devil's food cake with chocolate frosting and maraschino cherries all around the edge. She placed ten candles plus one for good luck on the top. And Davey drew a picture of a smiling yellow sun as a gift to his sister, who had miraculously stopped whining. Above the sun he wrote *Happy Birthday to my big sister Suzi*. Ah, the summer solstice!

HERB

"The ice cream man is here – the ice cream man is here!" Kit skipped with joy and hope into the backyard where Dad was sitting on the back steps, smoking a Pall Mall and thinking the day couldn't be any hotter. "Daddy! Daddy! Can we get some? Please?"

Herb searched his pockets. He knew if he found money for Kit, he'd have to find the same for Suzi and Davey, too. It was true that even though it was more expensive, the ice cream tasted better. It was so much more fun for the kids to follow the sound of the ice cream truck and buy a frozen treat than to scoop out a bowlful from the freezer at home.

That, Herb understood. All the neighborhood kids thrilled to the sound of the truck slowly winding its way through the streets, playing *Daisy, Daisy* over and over, enticing the children to hand over their allowances or beg their parents for twenty five cents for an orange popsicle or a chocolate covered, or a drumstick with walnuts on top.

Herb himself was partial to ice cream sandwiches, the ones with vanilla ice cream between two soft chocolate wafers. They were cold, sweet, and easy to eat. Herb had only a few teeth left in his mouth. His gums were tough and he could eat almost anything except corn still on the cob. But there were some things that weren't worth the trouble, and hard frozen ice cream was one of them.

Joyce would say "Put in your teeth, Herb." But the false teeth were made when Herb was much younger and slimmer, in the years after the war. They were tight and uncomfortable now; had been for many years. Herb wore his teeth only to formal occasions. With them in, he seemed handsome and robust. Without, his face had a sunken, haunted, poetic look.

"Hey, Dad – I want one too!" Glory shouted from her perch in the maple tree. Herb nearly keeled over in surprise. He didn't know that she was even around, much less a few feet away up in the branches. That Glory, he thought, startling me half to death.

Herb had slowly recovered from his stroke, a consequence of years of smoking two packs a day and the fright he got the day Davey got caught in the fire at the dump. Thank God for Penny, he thought. Herb was not a religious man, but the faith of his youth returned that day when Penny pulled Davey unharmed from the burning car.

He was hoping for another miracle, this time for Miriam. Her heart surgery had gone well, but then taken a turn when she contracted a stubborn fever. She was back at Mass General; things didn't look good.

Herb worried about more than his sister's health. The stroke had pulled an essential energy and confidence out of him. He hadn't worked over the entire winter. His union had taken up a collection, and Joyce had picked up some overtime at the plant. But not enough to make up for the loss of a man's paycheck. Sammy still had his paper route and Penny babysat every chance she could. But still, it wasn't enough.

He fished through his pockets and came up with eighty five cents. It would be enough for only three of his kids to get an ice cream. Herb wanted to give the world to all his children, not only the littlest ones. He started to cry. Ever since the stroke, his emotions were hard to control. It was as though every sad thought sat on top of his skin, waiting for the moment to stir up and cause a rash. He brushed the tears away and asked Glory to come down out of the tree.

Glory spent a lot of time up in the maple tree. She was a climber from way back, from the days many years ago when they moved to the house across from the field, a house with a real climbing tree.

You couldn't climb into the pines; they got sap all over you and were made for playing under, not climbing into. The maple tree in Glory's back yard was her favorite place to read and think. She'd bring an apple or two with her and read for hours without interruption.

She'd been reading the tale of Joan of Arc. It was an inspiring story, about how Joan talked to God and wore men's clothes into battle. About how, with God's guidance, she found the Dauphin, the future king of France, hidden in a room full of strangers. How she waged war against the Norman invaders, believing that she was absolutely right no matter the consequences. The Maid of Orleans, they called her.

Why are all the strong women of history and legend unmarried?

She hadn't reached the part about the real consequences for Joan. How they burned her at the stake. How she died for being a warrior woman. How she was made a saint but not for hundreds of years. Glory was reading the part about the triumphant Joan, blessed by God. A true heroine for a simpler, nobler time.

I feel noble, no – royal, and imperious. I shall bow to no one but my king, and then, only in the name of God. I feel quite sure of my position in the world, on top of my game. No one can stop me.

Gloria jumped down out of the branches. *Make way. Make way for the glorious Joan of Arc.*

"Glory, you're a big girl now," Dad said. "And you had a popsicle just a few days ago. I saw you and your friend Patty taking turns on a lime pop."

Crap, I know where this is going. Gloria had turned sixteen the winter before. She knew she was too old to put up a fuss, but that didn't stop her. "But Dad, that was Patty's. She just let me share it. I only got a few bites."

Dad bent his head. He didn't want his irritation to show. "Gloria, I'm buying ice creams for the peewees. I don't have money for you. Surely you're old enough to understand?" It was a question from a man who needed her compassion, who shouldn't have had to ask.

I don't understand. I am Joan of Arc, am I not? A great heroine, noble of spirit and touched by God. With fifteen hidden war scars on my breasts and thighs, symbols of my inner strength. I deserve better. I will never surrender, never give in to injustice.

"Dad, I want an ice cream. I don't see why I can't have one. Why do we have to be so poor? I can't even have a stupid ice cream. I hate you, I hate you!" Glory screamed at her father on the cement steps. She turned and ran to the maple tree.

My home base, the place I feel the most real, the most safe. I will not cry. True heroines never cry.

She looked back at her father. Dad was crumpled over with his head in his hands. He looked small and weak and ashamed. "I'm sorry, Glory," he mumbled. "I'm so sorry."

He was thinking, I can't do for my family. I'm not even a real man, I'm a failure. He couldn't look up.

~~~~~

Herb sat as if in a trance. He thought, I'm a failure...not a real man. In his mind he went back to the Normandy beaches, to Omaha beach, to the day they landed in the sand and rocks and salty shore. It was an invasion the size of which the world had never seen.

He recalled the beauty of the French hillside above the shore, how dense green hedges lined the horizon in perfect symmetry. He heard the gulls and thought of his native Dorchester, and remembered a girl he had left behind. How he and Joyce had kissed under the bandstand at Revere Beach and pretended they'd be true to each other no matter what happened, no matter how long the war would take.

He had thought of her, and how brave she'd be. And how brave he'd have to be to come back to her whole and alive. He had thought of her, and then reality hit.

Their battalion, the First Infantry Division, had left the relative safety of the transport ship. The men were moving on large landing crafts that pushed ahead on flat bottoms through the waters to the shore ahead.

Herb was a sergeant and the medic for his men. He was trained to do whatever it took to keep his wounded men alive until they could reach a medical facility and real doctors. A medic was, if he lived long enough, the very savior of the front lines. The difference between life and death for his men.

They moved close to the shore, and then the front of the boat flipped forward, dropping a ramp to the rocky bottom. Herb and all the men around him raced down into the icy cold water, their hearts pounding. Herb, who hadn't yet turned twenty two years old thought, the time for sightseeing is over. It was D-Day, and they all knew it was time to make history.

At that very moment, machine gun fire sprayed the ground in front of them. "Get down, get down!" shouted Herb. They weren't even out of the water and on dry land when soldiers started to die. Herb looked at the hillside, which had seemed so perfect and bucolic from the ship. He squinted in the sun. He saw what had not been apparent before – bunkers built down into the sandy beach on the hills. Bunkers filled with German soldiers out to kill them all.

There was screaming and bullets flying and explosions all around the men who had been told to take the hills or die trying. Herb didn't want to die, but he was no coward, and he knew the men were counting on him. "Push forward, push forward!" he screamed above the din. "We'll meet on the other side of that hill. Take some of them mother f___ing Krauts down along the way!"

A bullet rang out and right next to Herb, a man was down. It was Joe from Quincy. They had served in boot camp together.

Joe screamed in agony. His left leg was torn from the knee halfway up the thigh. Blood streamed out into the sand. Herb stopped and quickly pulled a tourniquet from his pack. He staunched the flow of blood the best he could. Then he lifted Joe up and supporting him under the arms, they moved to the shelter of a ditch that soldiers had just finished digging.

No sooner was Joe secured than Herb heard a huge explosion and screams coming from the front side of the ditch. He raced out toward the sounds, thinking, I've got to get to them. Another explosion rocked the ground, and Herb hit the dirt. When the dust settled a little, he looked around. There were six of his men lying dead in the sand. They were Carl, Mike, Joey C., Bill, Harvey, and Max. Max was a good friend of Herb's. They'd signed up for the army and had had good times together.

Herb's eyes filled with tears, but he didn't have time to mourn. He noticed an arm moving in the dirt. It was Nate, a kid only nineteen, and he was barely alive. Herb crawled over to him. Nate had taken shrapnel in the head and chest. Worse, his right arm had been blown clear off. Herb tried not to vomit, but he couldn't help himself. He knew he couldn't treat Nate in the sand – his wounds were too severe, beyond Herb's training. He knew he couldn't leave Nate to die. He picked him up and ran through the bullet shells to the safety of the ditch.

He was to save six frightened men all told that day, and two more the next before he himself was hit with an exploding shell. He caught shrapnel in eight places across his body. One flew right along the jaw and shattered most of his teeth. Herb would have died right there in the beauty of the French country side, in the glory of the hills, were it not for the bravery of some unnamed soldier who dragged him to safety.

Herb endured a long period of surgeries and recuperation to restore his health. He was awarded many medals of honor from the army. He received among others, a Purple Heart, a Bronze Star, and a Silver Star for his bravery. There was only one higher medal that could have been bestowed. Herb was a war hero among war heroes.

But all he could think of were the men he hadn't saved. A real hero would have gone out again. A real man would have risked his life to save a good kid like Carl, a buddy like Max. They were his men, truly his real family, and you do for your family.

He took his box of medals home. He showed them to his Mama and Pop, who were proud of him and overjoyed to have him home. He showed them to his favorite sister Miriam, and to all his brothers and sisters. He showed them to Joyce, his girl, who kissed him and agreed to marry him after a time.

Then Herb took his box of hard earned, well deserved medals of honor and stuck them in his dresser drawer. He never took them out again. He never, ever mentioned the war again in his life.

~~~~~~

Seeing her father so despondent, so helpless, so dreadfully low, Glory felt a stabbing sensation enter her heart, and a piercing realization. You would think that any good girl would have given her dad a hug and said, "It's alright. I didn't really want an ice cream anyway. Sorry for being such a pill."

But Gloria was not used to getting hugs, and she didn't give them out either. What she knew was guilt, yet she couldn't feel guilty. It was shame for her words, but not for her feelings. It was sorrow, but more.

It's as though I am the victor of a great battle. I just destroyed my enemy, an enemy I love. And though it causes me shame to admit it, because after all, he is my father, he will never be good enough. He is weak; I the superior.

And there is nothing he could say to make me change my mind. I can afford pity but not respect.

She would feel nothing but pity for him until the day he died.

Glory didn't realize the truth. To give her credit, she hadn't heard the story. And she hadn't read far enough — there was a cautionary tale between those covers. Joan was dead by age nineteen.

In Gloria's terrible anger, by her sixteenth year she had turned from doting queen to arrogant conqueror; from love to bitter hardness. She was way ahead of Joan. She still had three years left.

JOYCE

Joyce took the last drag from her cigarette and stubbed it out into her coffee cup. Where's an ash tray when you need one, she complained silently to the chipped and tortured mug.

She propped herself up in bed and looked around the room at the piles of her beloved books. They were mostly science fiction. She had Bradbury, Heinlein, Asimov, H.G. Wells, Vonnegut – all the greats. She loved sci fi for the adventure, the excitement of exploration, the unknown future. Most importantly, for the escape it offered from the deadening reality of motherhood.

Joyce started a new novel each Sunday morning once she'd gone through the *New York Times* and *Boston Globe*. It was a habit that helped keep her sane, in touch with a better world where children and cooking and family responsibilities were rarely mentioned.

Joyce liked books better than she liked most people, maybe even better than her own kids. In fact her books were like her children in many ways. She treated them the same. Just like her kids, her books were not well kept. Not put properly back on the shelf at night, not always read cover to cover or contents appreciated.

Rather, Joyce's books were dumped in piles surrounding her. Some with torn covers, others fallen behind the bookcase, pages splayed open with coffee stains. Or in a corner, dust covered and crawling with daddy long legs.

When she chose a book to read, she would devour it with pure pleasure. Nothing else would matter. Then, she'd throw it onto the discard pile where it would lie unseen, quite literally for years.

Joyce wasn't exactly what you'd call a good homemaker. She felt above it; that cleaning was perhaps meant for someone else but not her. She was comfortable in her mess and didn't care what anyone else thought about it. She wasn't bothered that her children were too ashamed of their home to bring friends to it. She'd say, "If they're really your friends, they won't care what your house looks like."

Though technically I have to admit that you have a point, Ma, it's mortifying to live in such filth. The pits. Really, hell on earth. I rarely bring a friend home. Not even Camille. Why don't you notice?

Joyce stretched and spotted a neglected title. She dug it out of the pile. Ah, she discovered, "Le Morte d' Arthur" – how did that get in here? She much preferred the future to the past. Joyce didn't believe in chivalry, knights in shining armor, silly legends like King Arthur, or a holy grail. Hell, she thought, there's absolutely nothing holy about this world.

~~~~~~

"Joycie, come inside and help your Auntie Annie," Mama yelled down the fire escape. "I've already told you twice. I don't want to have to say it again."

Estelle was not the yelling type, but today she was feeling more exasperated by the moment. With Friday night Sabbath only an hour away, the table wasn't even set. Not that they had nice things to make a beautiful setting.

She and her sister Annie had sailed from the old country on the boat to New York City with their mother Hannah, a few changes of clothing, and not much else. Ester (that was her name back then) had been only four when she came to Boston and didn't remember much from that time. But she did recall how her mother had cried and cried when they finally stepped off the trolley car at Ashmont Station. How Poppy had hugged them all so tightly, welcoming them to America.

They settled in Mattapan where rents were cheap. Poppy worked as a shoemaker. It was an honorable profession but they never got rich like the dream of America promised. He died of a stroke when Ester was ten and Annie thirteen. Hannah made both girls quit school, though she knew it was not what her husband would have wanted. She felt she had no choice. They had to make money to help the family survive, she told them.

Annie found work cleaning toilets at a downtown building. She had never been interested in learning or school work, or in finding a husband or moving away from her mother and sister. She had traveled enough for one lifetime, all the way from Poland and across the vast sea to a new world. That was quite enough for any girl; she was content to stay put.

Ester went to work in a fabric mill. She was pretty and petite and very smart, and wished she could have returned to school. Her mother would not allow it.

After a time she discovered there was more to life than the fabric mill. She dreamed of being a dancer on stage. She auditioned with an agent down at the Opera House, and was accepted for the chorus line. It was a risqué and improper career that Hannah refused to consider.

Ester thought her mother cruel in the extreme. She began to introduce herself as Estelle, a much fancier and more modern name than the ugly, old fashioned biblical Ester. She started flirting with boys on the street. When the war came, she tried to sign up to be a nurse and sail away to France. It would have been so romantic, Estelle dreamed, to care for wounded soldiers on the battlefront. Hannah said it was dangerous and utterly improper for a good girl to be a nurse. She forbade Estelle to go.

Estelle might have rebelled further and run away or come to

some other undesirable end. But fortunately for them all, by luck she met a handsome and intelligent young man from a good family.

Leo C__ and she fell in love three weeks before he shipped off to Europe with the First Infantry Division. They married after the war. Leo came back from his time at the front at Soissons physically unhurt. But he was moody and strange, changed from the young man Estelle had kissed goodbye.

Still, he was a good man. He rented a small corner store front on Columbia Road and stocked a kosher grocery. It was down the street from the apartment where they all lived. It was very hard work. He fed and clothed and housed them all.

~~~~~~

Years passed, and Poppy had died long ago. Bubbe Hannah was now an old and bitter woman. She and Annie crammed in with Estelle and Leo in their tenement apartment. They helped Estelle with Joycie, Jack, and Sadie, their three young children.

Altogether, they didn't have so much as an extra nickel or an empty corner of their crowded flat. With three hungry children to feed, even the Sabbath dinner was sometimes a thin affair. Estelle, Joycie's mama, often made matzo ball soup floating with carrots. At times, there was also heavy dark pumpernickel bread with cream cheese and juicy half sour pickles. On rare occasions, a roast chicken if Papa thought they could spare it.

Papa and Mama work night and day, it seemed to Joycie. They only take time out for meals and of course the Sabbath, which is required by the rabbi. Joycie sometimes wondered why, for all that work, their family couldn't eat whatever they wanted from the store. After all, it was theirs, wasn't it? But Mama said no, times are very tough. Our customers don't have enough money to pay us. None of us have enough. We can't eat what profits we have or we'll go out of business. Then where will we be?

"Joycie, where are you?" Estelle yelled. It was embarrassing to have such a disobedient daughter. All the neighbors knew that Joycie could be a real pill when she wanted to be. Praise God for my own beautiful Ruth (or Dottie, or Gert) they'd be thinking.

Joycie groaned and replied reluctantly, "Coming, Mama." She was only twelve, but already thinking of how to escape her exacting mother. Not to mention mean old Bubbe Hannah, and the drudgery of preparing for the Sabbath.

She thought that all the talk of religion and rabbis, of the endless rules and restrictions was for the birds. Who needs God, she wondered, when you have the moon and the stars and the big city with all the twinkling lights?

At least, as a girl, she wasn't forced to attend shul. She felt bad for her brother Jack. Starting at age seven, he had to accompany Papa to temple every Friday at sundown. And again Saturday morning, whether he wanted to or not.

Well, she couldn't feel too badly for him. After all, she was the house slave, cooking and cleaning and tending to the men and their duties, without any choice at all.

Joycie climbed back up the rusting metal fire escape and ducked into the bedroom she shared with Bubbe, Auntie Annie, and Sadie, her baby sister. "Give Sadie her bath," Mama commanded. "And change into your nicer dress. Hurry, it's almost sundown."

~~~~~~

"Ma, what are we having for supper?" Glory entered Ma's bedroom for the umpteenth time that morning. She sat on the edge of the bed and waited for Ma to look up from her reading.

"Gloria, I already told you – I'll think about it later," Ma replied with a heavy sigh. She loved her darling children but didn't particularly enjoy their constant interruptions. "We'll most likely have that roast." But it was hot as hell out. The thought of turning on the oven and heating up the whole house was more than Joyce could bear.

For crying out loud, I have to tell her. I can't let it go. "Ma," Glory began to say.

"Oh for God's sake, Glory, it's too hot to be pestering me! I'm suffocating in here!"

Ma flung off the bed sheet and swung her legs to the floor. She picked up her pack of cigarettes and matches, and trounced into the kitchen. Ah, she thought, it's a tad cooler in here. Joyce sat in her underpants and bra at the table and lit another cigarette. We'll probably have tuna with sliced tomatoes and cukes for dinner, she decided. Anything but cook.

Sammy ran in from the back door, sweating up a storm and looking for the pitcher of Kool Aid. He saw his mother and averted his eyes. It wasn't the first time he'd seen Ma in the kitchen in her underwear. He gulped down two tall glasses of his drink as he looked the other way, and then bolted back out the door. Thank God, he said silently and with great humility to the god of good fortune. Thank God none of my friends were with me today.

~~~~~~

Joycie sat with her arms folded across her chest. She was annoyed to no end. She had sat through the lighting of candles and the endless prayers, hadn't she? The only saving grace about the unbearable Sabbath routines was the meal. The past several months, she'd noticed, they'd had smaller and smaller amounts. But at least they weren't forced to eat the salmon patties and boiled potatoes that was their regular meal, night after night. We always have better food on Friday nights, she thought. So what's with tonight?

Tonight's dinner was lean, very lean. There was only soup – a thin chicken stock with some celery and carrots – and tea. No roast, no kugel, no boiled potatoes - not even a few pickles. No bread. Just soup.

She looked over at Mama, whose eyes were tearing up as she passed the bowls around. Papa sat hunched at the head of the table. He said, "Baruch Atah A-donai, E-lokanu Melech Ha-Olam. Blessed are You, Lord our God, King of the universe. Amen." Papa wanted everyone at the table to understand. They had already recited the Hebrew prayers, but Joycie didn't know what any of them meant. Girls didn't need to know Hebrew, just cooking and cleaning, Bubbe always said.

Joycie furiously eyed the soup bowls. She thought she deserved better than chicken stock for supper. She didn't know what God had to do with anything. She said to her father angrily, "I'm starving! Is this all we're having?"

Just then, Jack tipped Joycie's soup as he passed her bowl. The hot soup spilled all over her one nice dress. She flung her arm up to protect herself and hit the bowl. It went crashing to the floor.

Bubbe, who was sitting on Joycie's other side, reached out and slapped her wrist. She disliked her messy, argumentative granddaughter. That set Sadie to wailing, and Mama burst out crying. Papa stood up. He'd heard Joycie's outburst, but didn't answer her question. It was one for God, not him. Instead he said, "Here, my little Joyceleh, have mine." He brought her his bowl of soup and returned to his chair.

Leo picked up his cup of tea and sipped it sadly, thinking of the failure his life had become. How, despite his service as soldier, he wasn't much of a man. He couldn't even properly feed his own beloved family. The grocery store was in terrible debt. He wouldn't be able to pay next month's rent. The harder they worked, the more they owed.

Leo hated seeing his lovely wife and children go without. Estelle hadn't bought a new dress in years. He thought back to before the war, to those playful days when they had first met. How they danced and how he sang to her from his heart. "Daisy, Daisy, give me your answer do. I'm half-crazy all for the love of you."

He couldn't believe his luck, that someone as beautiful as Estelle could care for him. He loved her almost immediately. During that long, hard and lonely time when he was in France, she waited for him.

When he came home, he had nightmares about the shellings and the killings he saw. He couldn't get the pictures out of his head. Even now, the ugly scenes were with him. All the more reason to praise God for Estelle. She loved him through all those bad times, and loved him still. It was something of a miracle. He didn't believe he deserved her.

Leo grew more and more despondent as his mind recited the crushing burdens he carried. Rent ...food ...foxholes ...clothing ...new suit for Jack's bar mitzvah ...money ...heat ...not a real man ...family ...bullets ...blood ...debt ...hungry ...desperate. He listed his worries in his mind over and over.

Then, an idea filled his head. It was an awful idea, a rash and extreme idea, but it would work. He would wait until after the Sabbath. Leo lifted his face. He looked up to the One, to He Who Has No Name, and shouted his silent thanks.

~~~~~~

"But, Ma...listen." Glory was now fuming with annoyance. *Why can't my own mother pay me the slightest bit of attention? Especially when I have something I know you need to hear. Just because it's goddamn Sunday and you'd rather be reading about little green men invading Mars, you can't listen to me for one minute?*

"Alright, Gloria, what is it?" Joyce put her paper down. She loved her daughter's blazing eyes and fiery spirit. Just not now, not when it took her away from the peace she found in her reading.

"Don't you remember that today's the day Nannie and Aunt Sadie are coming on the bus? They'll be here in an hour or so."

Finally, for Hade's sake, relief. I finally got Ma's attention. Hell has frozen over. Hallelujah.

"Oh, Christ — I forgot all about it!" Ma jumped up out of her chair. She looked around. The house was a horrible mess. No one had cleaned in weeks. She knew she'd have to endure her fastidious mother's silent criticisms and disgusted stares. Estelle hated a dirty house.

Then she thought of something far worse — the roast. The roast wasn't Kosher. It wasn't goddamn Kosher.

She didn't have anything else to offer her mother and sister. She couldn't give them tuna out of a can, no matter how hellishly hot the air was around them. Mama and Sadie were traveling all the way from Boston. They'd have to walk to the bus stop on Columbia Road. Then they'd take a city bus to the Peter Pan Bus station, and then another bus ride an hour long just to visit for the afternoon. At six o'clock sharp, they'd reverse the trip on the one bus out of this god forsaken cow town. It would be a long day. They deserved better than canned tuna. They would hope for more from Joyce.

~~~~~~

It was Saturday evening, and all the prayers had been said. The candles had burned down to their nubs, the candlesticks put away, the prayer shawl folded. Sabbath, the holiest times of the year, even holier than the High Holidays, was over for another week. It was time for Leo to put his plan into action.

He took out the key that opened his desk. As man of the house, only he controlled the key, only he had access to the contents in the desk.

He carefully reviewed all his papers. There was the lease for the apartment, the lease for his grocery store. There were pictures of his beloved parents, may they rest in peace, and his sister Pearl, still in Hungary and waiting for her chance to cross the Atlantic.

There were birth certificates proving citizenship for all of his children – Joyce, Jacob, and little Sadie. A life insurance policy in good standing for five hundred dollars, to support his family should anything happen to him. His naturalization certificate. An honorable discharge from the army, and three medals of valor. A discharge from the hospital where he had recuperated from the exhaustion of the war and revived his mental health.

Leo counted what money he had been able to save over years of hardship. It came to fourteen dollars and sixty two cents. This was his bank. He wrote a note. "Five dollars for Jacob's bar mitzvah suit," it read. The rest would be up to them. He carefully arranged his papers, closed the desk, and put the key in the lock. They'll see it soon enough, he told himself.

He kissed his children good night, and told them to be good, just as he had done every night before. He sat for a cup of tea with Bubbe Hannah and Auntie Annie. They were remembering the old country before they came to America, and thinking of dear Poppy. Then he and his beautiful Estelle went to bed. He made love to her as though for the last time.

Estelle thought, we may be poor but we have each other, and that's enough. That night, she dreamed a glorious dream. They were all of them together, even Poppy, and they had taken the train from Boston to Revere Beach. They were swimming in the sea; happy and full of beef franks and crackerjack and root beer floats. Then they all mounted the giant Cyclone roller coaster, and screamed in delight as the monster flung them breathlessly through the salt air.

When Joycie awoke the next day, it was Sunday morning. Time to get the paper, she thought. No matter how poor they were, Mama and Papa had to read their papers. It was not negotiable. They had to have news of the world. Mama split the cost with Mrs. Saltsberg upstairs and Mrs. Nessel down. It brought the actual price each week to only a few pennies. It was a good system and worked well. Joycie was always the first up; it became her job to retrieve the paper.

This time, she took the fire escape. She ducked out her bedroom window onto the rusted landing. She turned to take the steps. There were white sheets pinned to the line up above. Mrs. Saltsberg probably hung her laundry last night, she thought.

It was the Christian Sabbath today. The city authorities, as rigid as the rabbis themselves, didn't allow a show of work on Sundays. It didn't matter if you were Christian, God forbid, or not.

She noticed some black clothing caught in the metal below. Mrs. Nessel's laundry, she thought. She took another step, then froze. Something was wrong, really wrong. Joycie took the next flight in an instant. She looked at the black clothing with a fear that she had never known before. It was Papa. He was hanging by his necktie from the fire escape railing.

Joycie struggled. She struggled with her fear. Her body moved one way, and then the other. She gagged and choked, and tried to run but she was paralyzed with the sight of Papa dead. She fell to the grated landing.

As the shock of the metal hit her knees, she finally let out a scream that would wake the whole neighborhood. She collapsed and lay on the grate, sobbing and heaving and wishing for all the world to leave her be, to let her escape from the madness of the day. Wishing for this horrible Sunday morning to end. She was only twelve, but she had seen enough reality for a lifetime.

Days later, after the funeral and awful week of mourning, Joycie's family was to learn another bitter truth.

It was not enough that the rabbi refused to bury Papa in the cemetery with full military honors. The rabbi said that Jews don't kill themselves, and when they do, they are punished by God for taking their own lives.

Therefore, Papa had to be buried on the edge of the cemetery, in shame. Papa's grave could not touch any other Jewish grave for fear of contamination. Papa, who in life, loved his faith more than most, was an outcast in death.

It was not enough that the rabbi insisted that Jacob, not yet ten, come to shul every morning for an entire year. "Every single morning for a year, without fail, before school or before your chores," Rabbi said, "to pray with the men to God for your father's forgiveness."

Jack did as he was told, and Bubbe with her harsh ways made sure of it. After that year was over, Jack never again set foot in the temple of the faith of his father. Never bar mitzvah'd. Never became a man in the eyes of an unforgiving God he hated with all his soul.

Those humiliations and tests of character and strength were not enough.

Mama and Bubbe brought the life insurance policy, in good standing for five hundred dollars, to the lawyer. The lawyer read through the document. He read it quite carefully. Then he put the paper down on his desk, took his handkerchief from his pocket, and wiped his eyes under his glasses.

"Mrs. C____," he addressed Mama with the utmost respect,

"there is a disclaimer in this policy. It states that should the insured commit suicide, the policy becomes null and void. Do you know what that means?" Mama shook her head. She had never heard such fancy language.

"It means that because your husband killed himself, the insurance company won't pay. The insurance is only for accidental death. It doesn't cover a man taking his own life."

Leo had tried the only way he knew to support and protect his family. He thought he was doing the right thing, the only thing to save them from starvation and financial ruin. But in the end, instead, his family was plunged into a debilitating poverty that would haunt them, like the sight of a father hanging by his neck, for the rest of their lives. The God of Abraham had spoken, and finally, He had had enough.

~~~~~~

With the threat of Nannie and Aunt Sadie approaching, Ma was strangely transformed. It was an odd thing, the hate and love she felt, both at the same time, for the family she'd yearned to escape.

This moment became Ma's to shine, to cast off the earlier funk of that hot and dreary Sunday morning. She threw on a housedress and pulled a comb through her hair, then called all the kids in from the yard. You'd think she was the one out on the front lines, the sergeant shouting orders to her men in the ditches.

"Herbie!" she commanded her husband who happened to be on the pot at the time. "Take the car, go to the delicatessen. Get some good gefilte fish and a jar of borsht. Don't forget the sour cream — oh, and some of those candied fruits my mother likes. And bring back something good for Sadie. She'll like a surprise. Take Sammy with you. Sammy, you're going for a ride. Kids! Come on, pick up and throw that stuff into the closets. They'll be here soon enough."

Herbie came out of the bathroom a little slowly. He was still recovering from the stroke and didn't do anything fast. He walked up behind Joyce and patted her on the bottom. Herb was an understanding man who loved his wife. He knew what Sundays were all about. "My little Joyceleh," he said, happy for once to see her smile.

PENNY

"Aw, Dad, do I have to take them with me?" moaned Sammy. "It's gonna mess up everything if I have to take them along! What will the guys think?"

Dad had purchased another old black Buick last spring. Sammy had the car for the first time since prom night. He and his friends Pete and Jimmy were going to drive to Nantasket Beach and ride all the rides at Paragon Park. They'd be there the whole evening and not come home until after the fireworks.

They had plans, big plans. They would, just by accident, run into Denise and her two best friends. Who, rumor had it, would be riding the roller coaster themselves that evening.

School was out and both Sammy and Penny had graduated from high school. But somehow, even though there were no classes to whisper in, notes to pass or lockers to hang out at, news got around fast in their small circles. Everyone knew how much Sammy liked Denise, even though he was going off to college in only a few months and Denise would be left working at the dry cleaner in town.

Denise wasn't so sure about who she liked, especially as she was an inch or two taller than Sammy. She had wanted a taller beau. But her mother said Sammy was a good catch. A college man, destined for success. Didn't the paper say he'd graduated number three out of the whole class? A brilliant boy, an Ivy Leaguer, maybe law school after that. Good enough by far for her under achieving daughter.

Then Denise told her mother the truth, that Sammy is Jewish.

"He doesn't look Jewish," her mother had replied. "He looked perfectly normal, handsome even, in his tux on prom night. And he was so polite. You must have heard wrong, Denise. You must be mistaken."

Denise told her mother there was no mistake – Sammy is Jewish. You don't have a name like Samuel when you're Christian, she'd said. That's a Jewish name. And she'd driven by his house last winter and had seen blue candles in the window, but no Christmas tree, no wreath on the door. She'd thought that was oddly strange, but then heard that Jews don't celebrate Christmas. She didn't know what Jews do celebrate, but it is some weird thing involving blue lights. They don't believe in Jesus, Denise had said.

Denise's mother didn't know how Denise knew such things, but she was shocked by the report. She instantly reconsidered her daughter's future. What had been a clear, smart scenario dissolved into a murky, uncertain view. And she wasn't about to incur the wrath of Father O'Brien. God forbid her daughter date a Jew.

"Oh...well," she said, "that Sammy, he is a bit on the short side. Maybe you should look for someone taller, someone you have more in common with. Like that nice Billy what's-his-name. He's a good looking boy, and off to the state college in the fall. I hear he'll be living at home instead of the dorms. He should be around a lot. You know what, Denise honey, instead of you going to the beach, why don't we do a little shopping tonight? Just the two of us." Denise's mother wasn't a bigot. She just had a strong maternal instinct. She only wanted the best for her daughter.

~~~~~~

Sammy couldn't wait. They'd meet up with Denise, the love of his life, and her two gorgeous friends. They'd ride the roller coaster and the Ferris wheel. Sammy would spring for cotton candy and if he was lucky, he and Denise'd take a walk on the beach and watch the tide go out. Anything can happen once we're walking on the beach, Sammy thought.

But not if he had to take along the ugly and the crazy brigade, his two idiot sisters. Even if Denise never showed up, the guys would have a great time. But not if Penny and Glory tagged along. "They'll ruin my whole night, Dad. I want to be with my friends. It just isn't cool to take sisters along."

Herb was sweeping out the garbage that had built up under the kitchen table. He listened to Sammy whine. He thought of his own sister Miriam. How wonderful it would be if Miriam were well enough to take a ride to the beach, to breathe the salt air and ride the Ferris wheel. To eat ice cream and French fries, and watch the fireworks over the water.

Herb had grown up in a proper Kosher home, a clean house, and there were times he got sick of the mess they all lived in. Once in a while, he got sick of Sammy. Today he had had enough of Sammy to last, it seemed, a lifetime. He didn't care what Joyce's views were on corporal punishment. He was ready to raise the straw broom in his hands and take a whack at Sammy. Chase him around the house if necessary (because it was true that Sammy was quick) and give him a good smacking once he caught him.

Why have we always favored him? he wondered. Penny is such a good dependable girl, and Glory just as smart. For God's sake, Sammy is a man, eighteen years old. There were men that age in Normandy, men he commanded in battle. No one whined. No one carried on, they just did their duty.

And Sammy knows that Glory and Penny are having troubles. Maybe a nice time together at Nantasket would make them both feel better, heal whatever wounds there were between them. You never know how things will turn out if they give it a chance.

Herb was finally back at work, almost a year after the stroke. The money wasn't quite so tight; the man size paycheck a big relief. Herb was proud of Sammy for getting a full scholarship to college, and of Penny for being the first girl on either side to go to college at all. He wanted the best for all his children. Herb wanted his kids to feel free, to drive into the wind, to experience their youth and strength and optimism.

But he also hoped they'd appreciate what they had, even if it was only a little. He hoped Sammy and Davey down the line would never have to go to war as he did. He prayed to the old Hebrew God for this war to end before Sammy could be drafted into it.

And all he asked was for the complaining to stop, for the seed of maturity to grow. An eighteen year old couldn't be expected to grasp the full meaning of life, that's true. But was it too much to ask for a little understanding?

Sammy, though, wouldn't give it up, and finally Herb had enough. Whining was the cardinal sin – or in words even Jews could understand, the unforgivable offense. "Sammy," he said with admirable restraint, "give me the keys. Tonight, you're not going anywhere."

~~~~~~

Later that evening, Penny, who also had her driver's license and now use of the Buick, drove to the lake at the edge of town with her best friend Naomi. Dad had said she could take the car if she also drove Glory and her friends Patty and Beth, who were all looking for a ride.

Penny wasn't talking to Glory, but she wanted the car and grudgingly agreed. They would watch the bonfire that the junior class had planned for a time after school let out when no one could get in trouble for it. It was a tradition, an annual event for rising seniors that everyone in high school attended except for graduated seniors who had moved on to celebrations at the Cape or Horseneck or Nantasket Beach. There'd be hundreds of kids at the lake, all young and energetic and excited about the summer season that had just begun. There'd be a mountain of a bonfire, too big for safety's sake.

Penny and Naomi knew it wasn't fashionable for them to go to the underclassmen event. As graduates, they should have been somewhere else, anywhere else along the coast of southeastern Massachusetts.

On the beach, not here. If you can leave, you do, was the mantra of every teen old enough to drive in this inland cow town. The beach was the place to be. But Penny and Naomi didn't get many invitations, and they'd run out of money for trips to the shore. Penny had spent every dime she'd ever saved on her prom dress and shoes. It was worth it, but now there was nothing to do except earn more babysitting money for college. Penny set her sights on college, where she was sure her life would be different and much, much better in every way. "Be back at the car by midnight," was all Penny would say to Glory when they arrived at the lake.

Penny and Naomi walked over to the bonfire which was set on the small sandy shore of the lake. Teenagers were throwing everything they could think of into the fire. They brought wooden crates, broken furniture, old signs and wooden tool handles and wheel barrows, and anything else not nailed down to stoke the fire. Flames leaped out of the huge burning pile. Sparks flew everywhere.

They walked all around the perimeter of the growing fire, from one edge at the water, through the sand to the other side. They watched the red and orange flames build a monumental force. The teens crowded together, all eyes on the fire, pushing and shoving to get the best view, to guard their territory, to establish who was who.

Then a splash of sparks lit up the dark sky and fell on those too close to the flames. Penny was one of them. "Ouch, ouch!" she cried as she moved quickly back, swatting at the spots on her arm where the sparks had landed. She backed up right into a group of freshman boys.

"Hey, didn't you just graduate?" one of them snidely remarked. "Yeah, she's too dumpy to be at the beach. Afraid of what she looks like in a bathing suit!" another said. "All Jews are ugly. This one's piggy Penny!" a third yelled through the crowd. The boys looked meanly at Penny. They laughed loudly, proud of their sarcastic wit.

"Jerks!" Naomi retorted. It was a good try, but she'd never been much at quick replies.

Idiots. Penny shook her head. They could taunt her all they wanted — it was just more proof that this place was like a jail sentence. She and Naomi, the only friend it seemed she had in the world, walked away and sat down under a pine tree. Penny rubbed her arm. She watched the flames. Their mystery drew her in and she became mesmerized by the sight. They reminded her of something that happened long ago, a time she'd never forgotten but had put out of her mind, for safety's sake.

~~~~~~

Penny was so excited. It was the first time ever that she would watch baby Gloria all on her own. Daddy had taken Duke to the vet. Duke had run away and come back days later covered in ticks and burrs. The vet wanted to put him out of his misery, but Daddy said no. He's a good dog — clean him up. Mama said Penny was a big girl, five years old now, and old enough without Duke's help to play outside with Glory while Mama took a nap.

Mama needed to rest. She had been sad for a long time. Daddy had said they were getting a new baby, even smaller than Glory who wasn't quite three. It would be either a new brother or a new sister. Penny had hoped for another sister because she already had a brother, and even though he was her twin, she didn't like him much.

But then Daddy said the baby wasn't coming. The new baby had gone away before it had a chance to be born, to come out of Mama's tummy. That made Daddy sad, and Mama even more sad. Penny wondered where the new baby went, but she couldn't ask Mama, because Mama stayed in her bed and read books all day long. She smoked cigarettes and came out only to use the bathroom and make dinner for Daddy by five.

Penny knew she would be a good babysitter for Glory. She already knew how to make peanut butter and jelly sandwiches. She knew how to pour the milk. She had figured out how to turn on the stovetop for grilled cheese. She could even make a can of Campbell's chicken noodle soup for lunch, though it hurt her hands to turn the can opener. Penny was quite self-sufficient and felt perfectly ready to be Glory's substitute mother.

They gathered some supplies and headed out to the giant pine trees that grew on the edge of their yard. Glory brought her best bear, Teddy. Penny brought a picnic blanket, four little tea cups, a story book, and her favorite doll, the one with the curly red hair and ceramic face.

Penny loved her doll, but she couldn't name her because she knew the doll wasn't real. Not like her sister Glory, who had dark hair and violet eyes and looked just as pretty as any doll. Penny understood that real was better. She knew how to read because Mama had taught her, and now she was teaching Gloria. Only real girls can read, though dolls and teddy bears can listen, of course. They would have tea and read their story under the pines. They would have a glorious time.

Penny and Gloria settled in. "Would you like some tea, my dear?" Penny asked Glory.

"Yes, please," Glory answered. Even at almost three, she was always polite. "But I think dolly wants hot chocolate. I don't think she likes tea."

"Alright then, we'll all have hot chocolate. I agree, it's much yummier." Penny poured the pretend hot chocolate into a cup.

Just then, Sammy charged through the pine needles. He banged into Penny and knocked over the cup. The pretend hot chocolate sprayed onto Penny's arm and scalded her skin.

Penny rubbed at the spot and began to cry. "Sammy, you're always so mean. I hate you, I hate you!"

Sammy laughed. He was only five but he already knew how to spur his sister into a tizzy. It was easy to make her cry. You didn't need a plan of attack. Just barging in on her make-believe would do it. It was so easy — a piece of devil's food cake.

Girls, Sammy thought. Girls are stupid crybabies. You don't have to do anything and they'll be weepy and carry on for no good reason.

He ran off into the woods, to the spot where the guys had their fort and campfire. It was an opening between a stand of oaks where no grass grew. He and some of the neighborhood boys had built a ring of stones and dumped sand into it. They lit campfires and hung out. So long as they kept the fire low, they figured their dads would never find it. Their fort was their sanctuary, a place where no girls were ever allowed.

Penny rubbed her arm and thought about Sammy. She wondered why he hated her so much. She wondered what she had done to deserve the way he treated her.

Mama and Daddy liked Sammy. They laughed at all his jokes. They thought it was funny when Sammy said to Penny, "You don't really belong to our family. You're adopted. Someone left you on our step, and Ma felt so bad for you she brought you in." Penny knew that couldn't possibly be true – she and Sammy were twins. But her parents laughed anyway. They thought he was the best thing ever.

No, it must be something she did. There must be something wrong with her. It was her, not him.

Glory jumped up. She said, "Penny, I have to go. I have to go bad." She stood before Penny, wiggling and crossing her legs.

Penny didn't think Glory could make it back into the house in time. "Okay Glory. Go into those woods. Make sure no one can see. Pull your pants down."

Glory ran off into the woods. She looked for a bush or a tree, or someplace that was hidden so she couldn't be seen. She ran deeper into the woods.

Penny waited for Glory. She waited and waited, but Glory didn't come back. What was taking so long?

She straightened up under the pines. She wrapped her doll and Teddy into the picnic blanket and said, "It's time for a nap." She neatly lined up the tea cups, and placed them on the story book that had yet to be read. She looked around her pine needle room. Everything is neat and clean, she thought, everything in order.

Mama was right, she was a big girl, she could be trusted.

Trusted with what? It came back to her in a flood. This isn't real. Where is my real baby? Where is Gloria?

Penny ran off into the woods frantically searching for her sister. "Glory!" she called out, "Glory, where are you?"

Meanwhile, Sammy ran to the campfire and found his friends. They were throwing darts at an old target they'd nailed to a tree. "Hey Sammy!" they yelled. "Want to play?"

Sammy had something else on his mind. He had to go bad, really bad. He said "I bet I can pee from here right into the fire!"

The boys crowded around to check Sammy's boast. He took his best shot but missed by half a foot. He got closer and almost hit the rocks. He moved closer still and his stream finally hit a hot rock. They watched it sizzle. The guys had a new game. Suddenly, they all wanted to try.

They stood in a circle around the campfire and opened their pants. Each one tried to outdo the other. There was Tony, a seven year old from down the block, and Bobby who lived next door. There was Jeff, five like Sammy but tall and husky, and Chris, Jeff's brother. There was Sammy of course, and Butch, the old man in the felt hat who hung out with them at the fort and sometimes slept in the oak tree.

They were pissing and laughing and pissing some more at the open flames. Then they heard a yell, a girl yelling "Glory, where are you?"

"That's just my stupid sister Penny. You can forget about her — she'll never dare to come here." Sammy was quite certain. The man was not so sure. He zipped himself up and disappeared into the woods. The boys kept pissing into the fire. It was great fun.

Penny burst into the clearing. Her face was red from running. She looked at Sammy and the rest of the boys. They were laughing and peeing into the fire. Penny looked around. "Is Glory here?" she asked.

"Of course not, you dumb bell. Can't you see we're busy?" Sammy said.

Tony said, "Hey Penny, you want to play?"

Penny didn't know what game they were playing, but they were laughing and having fun, so she said yes, she did want to play.

"Okay then, pull your pants down. The game is to see how far away you can be and still pee into the fire." Tony was interested. He'd never seen a girl's pee pee before.

Sammy thought with an irritated sigh, why did Tony ask Penny to stay? Who cares about a dumb old girl anyway?

Penny took off her shorts and underwear with the tiny flower pattern. She squatted next to the campfire and tried to send her pee toward the rocks. The boys saw her naked body and began to laugh at her pitiful try. She wasn't anywhere near as good as a boy at this game. Why did she bother?

She hadn't come close. She turned around and backed herself in to try again. The boys burst out laughing at the sight of her bare bottom. Penny turned red with embarrassment. She couldn't get her pee into the fire, and everyone was laughing at her.

She took another step back. She'd show them – she was just as good as any boy. She backed up right to the ring of rocks. She squatted down, let out her last stream of pee, and sat right down on a burning hot rock.

The boys roared with laughter. They couldn't control themselves. To give them credit, they didn't see Penny's skin hit the hot rock. All they saw was a bare naked girl, pissing and squatting in front of their eyes. It was the howl of a lifetime.

Penny stood up and screamed in pain. The alarming sound sent Tony and Bobby, Chris and Jeff running out of the woods like frightened deer.

Sammy zipped up. He didn't know what got into Penny – she was always crying and carrying on. He laughed thinking about the peeing game.

Penny screamed and cried until Mama, awakened from her nap and Daddy, who had just returned from dropping Duke off at the vet, came running.

Daddy looked at his half naked daughter and demanded, "What's going on here?"

Mama said, "Where are your clothes?"

They didn't see Penny's burn. They were too confused to grasp Penny's humiliation. All they saw was Sammy laughing, trying hard to stop.

"It was just a game," said Sammy with a new innocence. "Just a silly little game."

Mama smiled a little and shook her head. It was true that Penny could cry without any provocation at all, it seemed. Then Mama noticed - Gloria was missing. "Where's your sister, Penny? You were supposed to be watching her."

Penny was crying too hard to answer. "Put on your clothes, please! And stop that crying," Mama said.

For crying out loud, a little game of doctor never hurt anyone, Joyce thought. It was perfectly normal, a natural part of growing up. She'd seen a toy medical kit at Woolworth's Five and Dime. Maybe she'd buy one for Sammy. He'd make a great doctor someday.

It was then that Sammy, plenty smart Sammy, knew he could get away with almost anything when it came to Penny. Penny was weak and stupid; he, strong and crafty. She can cry all she wants and I won't get blamed, he realized. He'd be taking full advantage from that moment on.

They went looking for Glory and found her at the edge of the yard. She was hugging a pine branch and crying for her mother. And she was naked, completely naked.

That was the night that Penny started wetting her bed. The day she realized that it was she who was no good, that her body was a laughing matter. The evening she learned the truth – that boys are better, that Sammy would always be better.

That no matter how hard she'd try, she'd never be first in her parents' eyes. They couldn't even see her pain, that's how much they loved Sammy more. There was nothing else to say, no words. No way around the truth, the not-so-secret of a lifetime. It was a bitter lesson for a five year old girl child.

~~~~~

Penny heard the snapping, crackling bonfire. It brought her out of her reverie. She stood up and brushed the pine needles and dirt off her shorts. "Come on Naomi, let's go," she said. She had seen enough. She was done.

They looked for Glory and found her down by the water. "Gloria, we want to leave. Can you and your friends find another ride?" Penny asked.

Glory looked at her sister. She saw a sadness, a weariness in her eyes. She answered, "Sure Penny, don't worry about me. I'll find my own way home."

Penny turned and walked toward the car. She smelled the pines and the cool night air. She heard the frogs croaking from the swampy edges of the water. And cicadas chirping away in the trees.

She might have looked around and seen her country town,

Mother Nature in all her glory. But Penny wouldn't look around, not even a little, and she'd never look back. She'd leave her past behind because it was the only thing to do. Because she needed to move on, to drive into the wind, to experience her youth and discover her strength.

And for the first time ever, college bound, she'd savor a hint of her future to be. It was a sweet taste, the taste of freedom.

GLORY

Glory watched as Penny and Naomi left the bonfire.

I can take care of myself. I don't need her — I don't need anyone at all.

It was true that Penny and Naomi had each other. Patty and Beth had the same. They were best friends, and though they'd included Glory in most everything they did after Camille kicked her down and dragged her through the mud, still, Glory had changed.

And not for the better. Gloria used to be fun and so energetic. She'd laugh till she'd choke and be hugely entertaining. She'd howl at the wind and moo at the cows and not worry a bit about how she looked doing it.

Glory hadn't been afraid of anything or anyone, not math or science or French or any of the teachers. She'd be drenched in the rain and still dare the lightning to strike. She'd been inspiring, a leader, a person you couldn't help but follow. There were worries inside her, but she didn't let them show. She'd had the confidence of a queen.

That was before. Now she was sullen and got defensive and angry if you said one word out of line. She pulled back if you even came near. Glory pretended her fairy tale thing more and more — the latest was Joan of Arc. She'd stick her nose up in the air to show herself superior, and act like she didn't really want to be with you, like she'd rather be alone.

And her clothes and hair were outrageous. It was as though she was in a crazy kind of mourning or something, like there'd been a death, like there was no life after Camille, and she was punishing herself for it. Her violet eyes were ice and cold, cruel.

Both Patty and Beth understood. It was hard, so difficult to lose your best friend in the whole world. But Glory was tough and getting tougher to be around, and they were young. You had to give them credit for sticking with her as long as they did. They were happy they had each other, secure in their own undying friendship.

"We'll catch up with you later, Glory," they said. They thanked Penny for the ride and walked together toward the giant fire on the edge of the lake. Soon they were lost in the crowd.

The hell with them, Glory thought bitterly. *They can go flip Hades the finger for all I care.* She turned and walked in the other direction. The opposite from Beth, opposite from Patty, her two last friends, the last to care.

She gazed at the bonfire and thought of the summer sun.

How I hitched into Boston just the other day. How the glare of the sun in the trucker's eyes had blinded him for a moment, how we'd almost crashed into the guard rail. It was lucky – he'd had his hand on my leg for balance; I grabbed the wheel and turned us back onto the pavement until he could recover his sight.

It's pure luck I have a body so many men want to touch, so many seem to need. Like the guy on Tremont Street who confused me for a street walker, who offered me thirty bucks to have sex. When I said no, you're confused old man, he looked sad as he walked away, as though he had missed the experience of a lifetime. I would have been so lucky to be with you, he seemed to be thinking.

And it would have been lucky if I could have gotten a job at the Playboy club on the corner of Boylston. I figured I could go in on afternoons and take the late bus home. I inquired, but the man told me I'm too young. Try again in a couple of years, he had said, but not before he stuck his hands up my top and down my shorts and felt my private parts. Evaluating my curvy figure for the job, I guess. It's lucky there are so many gorgeous young girls in the world, he seemed to think, and that you are one of them who happened into my office today.

Glory had reconsidered after her encounter with the slime bucket manager. *It would be stupid to wear a bunny outfit anyway, especially the puffy cotton tail on the back. I feel lucky I thought it through. Because queens don't wear ridiculous costumes to attract their suitors. They know their strengths. Queens don't have to wear anything; they are sexy enough just the way they are.*

You don't have to wear anything...

Glory thought back to the day she was lost in the woods.

And the man in the felt hat took off my clothes and touched me everywhere and put his pee pee on mine and sprayed all over me. That hadn't felt lucky. Maybe it was because I wasn't yet a queen. I was so small, I wasn't even a princess. He made me cry, and I hate to cry. Penny cried that day. I wonder if the man took off Penny's clothes too, if he went to the bathroom on her, too.

She thought about the snowy day.

The day I was so cold I couldn't walk back to the pine needle house. How the same man in the felt hat picked me up and almost carried me away. I couldn't fight him, I was so cold and tired. Duke was there that time — I feel lucky for Duke.

What a good dog Duke was. I wish he hadn't tried to follow me into the field. I wish he hadn't been killed trying to cross. That street is unlucky, the field too. The field makes me puke, it makes me want to throw up just thinking about it.

Gloria started to shiver, recalling the field and the woods beside it.

And the carnival and the man who ran the merry-go-round. It all comes back to me, the feeling of the hard bark of the oak tree against my back, how I hit my head on a root and threw up. How the man...how the man...Gloria didn't know what the man had done.

I only know that it was wrong, really wrong. I remember coming out of the woods, covered in dirt and blood and pine needles. I lost my money and walked home through the gate and...

The gate.

Strange, I recall running through the gate, not walking. I had definitely run. Because stones were hitting me on my back and my head and the backs of my legs. Rocks were biting my bare feet as I ran to escape the sweating crowd of boys, the steaming bleachers.

And the bleachers, where cruel Billy had tested my resolve and pushed me under the steely steps when I wouldn't do as he pleased. Where he'd mocked my virginity and left me like garbage and told me I would never be good enough. Where I'd limped home and wished I'd never been born.

My virginity...such a liability, so uncool in a world of free love. When I got home, I branded myself in pain. Fifteen years, fifteen cuts. An eye for an eye. A way to say, I hate who I am. Impulsive acts of aggression against myself, against my very being.

But in a strange, perverse way, they were also symbols of strength, a way of releasing the deeper pain. They were signs of my determination, a chance to regroup, to pause, to rethink what would come next.

Only virgins have real power, of that I am quite sure. Look back at history if you have any doubt. I couldn't give it up, certainly not to the likes of Billy. Robin Hood, maybe, though he already has a girlfriend. Sir Walter, perhaps, but he's always sailing off somewhere. King Richard of Lionheart fame – well, now you're talking. But come to think of it, he led the Crusades and killed all the Jews, all the infidels in his path. And Lancelot - no, a little too good looking, too stuck on himself, and too hung up on Miss Perfection, the all sweetness and light and ivory and pink Guinevere. So obsessed, he sabotaged his best friend, Arthur.

Hmmmm...King Arthur. Nothing to fault there. Worked to promote peace among the knights by building a round table where everyone was equal, though he failed because of course knights prefer to fight. Tried to build a nation of equals. That shows real character. A man before his time.

Sure, he loved Guinevere, the idiot princess, the pretty face. But a king is only a man, and all men are foolish around pretty girls. Give it some time, he'll snap out of it. Maybe someday he'll even prefer a queen with dark wild hair and a way of speaking her mind. A girl with violet eyes who can stand up for herself.

King Arthur - a humble, courageous, intelligent, only slightly flawed king to match a proud and gloriously imperfect queen. If only I could find him, now that would be lucky.

Someday, he'll be oceans away, hidden in the hills of Camelot. He'll send news from across that sea, good news, and it will be news of a brand new world, where I can be free to go wherever I want, whenever I want. It will be a world worth waiting for. Virgin territory. And no dumb creeps will stop me from getting there.

Gloria smiled just a little. It wasn't quite the smile of a lifetime, but it was good enough. It would do.

It will do, but I figure it will be a long wait, oceans of time, before King Arthur comes my way. It could be eons of time. And the fire, the bonfire is right in front of my eyes. Here, right now.

Her violet eyes stared at the hill of flames.

How long could anyone expect to wait for Camelot, for friendship, for love to arrive? Even companionship comes dear — when everyone you've known, even your own sister who is older and should know better, has abandoned you to the fire.

Joan was alone, Joan was brave and endured the flames. She was forced into them — they tied her up and bound her to the fire. But maybe it was for the best. Maybe Joan wanted it that way. Because the only friend Joan had was God. She was alone, so alone, and maybe she wanted to be with God.

Maybe she allowed herself to endure the fire so she could finally have a best friend who wouldn't go away, someone who cared so deeply for her He'd never give her up. He'd never think she was psychotic or a liar or a boyfriend stealer or a lezzie. He'd never force her to the ground and commit unspeakable acts or stone her because she was alone watching a baseball game when apparently she shouldn't have been. Joan was lucky to have God for a friend.

She walked closer to the flames.

I don't have God. I don't pray to the blue lights, or the cigarette gods, or the god of good fortune, or even to the goddess Persephone who raises the cruel spring.

It isn't Persephone's fault the spring brings chaos and disharmony. She ate three of Hades' pomegranate seeds — big deal. That's no reason to bind her to hell. That's no reason to give up on her. Hades is the mean one, the gross and disgusting pig of an underworld god. Persephone isn't much more than a child, Hades, though she looks adult. She's just a girl, Hades. Leave Persephone be.

Glory moved to a spot where the sparks flew straight out into the night air. She raised her hand to the sparks, and let them hit her fingers. She felt tingles but no pain.

Not much more than a child...Kit and Suzi are still children, and of course Davey, too. Sweet little Davey, my beautiful blond brother. So much cuter than any of my sisters. Well, Kit has beautiful dark hair and Suzi's is golden brown — they're both so lively and pretty. They have each other and they've never needed me. I'm not a part of their lives. And Davey is small, I love him so much, but I'll be gone long before he's grown. He'll have to do without me.

What would the world be like without me in it? What if I flung myself into the fire? The headlines might read, "A Joan of Arc for Modern Times." Or, "Friendless Girl Child Finds Out If God Is Real." No, more likely, "Crazy

Girl Who Has No One Kills Herself In Teen Bonfire." "Tsk, tsk," Mrs. Fournier might say, "What's wrong with these kids today?"

What if I waited and didn't throw myself into the flames? What if I waited until Penny and Sammy went off to college? Maybe Ma and Dad wouldn't even bother to tell them, to say I was gone. It would spare their feelings and anyway, what's done is done. Que sera, sera. Sammy would be too busy competing on varsity track and getting all A's to notice. He'd be in his Ivy League and too ashamed to mention his insane sister to anyone. He'd forget by Thanksgiving.

Penny might feel sad...yes, Penny might feel sad but it would serve her right to be sad because after all, haven't I been a good sister to her all these years? Why did she think I was at fault on prom night? Why does everyone think I'm the one doing something wrong? Sure, I've done some things that were wrong and dumb, maybe lots of things. But hasn't everyone?

How would I kill myself if it wasn't going to be by fire, the Joan of Arc method? Obviously, beheading is out of the question. And savages are unreliable — you have to usurp their land or do something to tick them off before they'll strike. Maybe I'll take a rusty razor blade and slit my wrists. No, that might hurt. I believe I'm done with cutting.

I could climb the maple tree right up to the top, as far as the limbs could hold my weight, and jump. But the maple tree isn't all that tall, and probably the branches would catch me and cushion my fall. I'd end up with broken arms and legs, not dead, which wouldn't do at all.

Here's an idea. I'll bide my time and wait for the right moment. Waiting, it seems, is my fate. I'll climb so high and jump so far, there'll be no mistaking the outcome. I'll pray to Mother Nature — can't hurt, I'll give it a try. Her laws prevail anyway, there's no point in fighting. In all Her glory, the simplest, most elegant, primal law — gravity. Yes, that will definitely do.

MOON LANDING

Glory felt the heat of the day land on her skin. It stuck like Elmer's glue. She couldn't shake it. A slimy sweat surrounded her and followed her wherever she went. There was no escape.

The peewees were in their swim suits, running through the lawn sprinkler that Dad had set up in the back yard. They were laughing and shouting, dripping wet and happy to race back and forth through the curtain of water that seemed icy cold compared with the ninety five degree air. It was the hottest day any of them remembered, certainly one for the record books.

Glory was too old to run through the sprinkler in her bathing suit, or so she was told. Around about fifth grade Ma had said that she was too grown up to run around half naked. It was one thing at the beach, or at a friend's pool. But not on the street, not in your open backyard where everyone could see.

Ma, who considered herself a citizen of the world so to speak, was strangely old fashioned when it came to her own kids, especially the well-developed female ones. There were just some things a good girl didn't do, and parading yourself in all your glory for the whole world to see was one of them.

Maybe that was why a year or more had passed, and no one had noticed Gloria's scars. No one had seen the ugly lines on her thighs or the jagged breaks against her breasts.

Not one of them had looked, really looked at Gloria. Not even Penny, who shared a bedroom and might have seen at least one of her sister's fifteen cries for help. Not Sammy, who ignored Glory as much as possible, hoping to tune out the crass remarks he heard around the locker room. Not Dad, always annoyed and uncomfortable around his pretty daughter. And least of all Ma, the mother who might have paid attention but didn't.

Honestly, there were so many things to think about, so much to occupy one's mind. There was the mortgage…food for eight…sneakers and coats and shoes and pants for ever growing children…college loans and Vietnam and protests in the streets…heart surgery and a sister-in-law's last days…taxes, paychecks, money, electricity. One couldn't see it all.

A daughter's cutting pain could go unnoticed with other children to tend. A sister's torn miseries might easily remain unseen when you weren't even talking to her. An almost grown child's razor blade lament could be overlooked or forgotten when, after all, it was old news. And how could you pay attention to the ordinariness of life when history was in the making?

And it was the event of a lifetime, of a hundred thousand lifetimes. It was July 20 in the year 1969 - the first time ever in the history of humankind that a man would walk on the moon.

The Apollo 11 lunar module. Neil Armstrong, Buzz Aldrin, Michael Collins. They were the talk of every conversation, the images behind every thought, everybody's greatest heroes. *The Eagle has landed,* Armstrong said. *That's one small step for man, one giant leap for mankind.* A human footprint on the surface of the moon, an inconceivable fete. Of course no one could think of anything else.

They huddled around the black and white television set just like everybody they knew in their old cow town. Probably everyone in southeastern Massachusetts was watching dumb founded, speechless, witnessing this unworldly event unfold. Perhaps all of Massachusetts, every last person from Cape Cod all the way to the Berkshires, strained to see the men on the moon through their magic viewer, their TV screen.

Herb was overwhelmed. It was like a chant or a prayer, an homage to an old angry God who had suddenly cast a softening moonlit glow on His people. That's how many times Herb shook his head and said, "I never thought I'd live to see the day a man walked on the moon. Never thought I'd live to see the day."

He thanked God for this softening, for allowing Miriam, too, to live to see history in its creation. He phoned her, she in her last days in her sick bed, he pacing back and forth. Both so anxious to connect, to see the moon together through new eyes, to make their final peace. When he hung up, Herb sobbed cries of a lifetime for all the bad and all the good that was his life.

And in fact they were all quite stunned and beyond words with the brilliance of the moment. Was this just an astounding technological victory, an update on Sir Walter's ships sailing across the sea? Or was it a discovery of a new and untested world?

Perhaps it was the end of an era, the end of time as we know it, of a time when people had limits and old ways and weights placed on them so they could barely move forward. So even the brightest and best could only inch ahead.

Or maybe it was the beginning of time, a time of anti-gravity, of breaking free from the old constraints, of leaping lightness, of acceptance and tolerance for new ideas.

Perhaps it was the courage of three strong men, or maybe it was yet another exclusion of the female side. It could have been a way of saying, only men are good enough to undertake such a dangerous journey, only men smart enough to defeat all odds. It might have meant, we are all good enough - we men are paving the way for all to come.

It could have been - there may be savages ahead, unknown and untold in the history of humankind. Deadly savages like the vacuum of space, a finite oxygen supply. The likelihood of crashing, of not having enough fuel to return. Of dying an awful death, of never seeing family and friends again. Of drifting in space for an infinity of time.

One small step for a man, because a woman would be too weak and inferior to survive it. A woman couldn't bear up under the strain of G forces. A woman doesn't have the intellect or the instinct or the strength. It would be a man's footprint in the lunar dust, not a woman's – that was as it should be, as everyone knew it should. It wouldn't even be a question.

Or, the message may have been different. It may have been that the gender didn't matter. That, as a great man once said, the content of one's character was the key.

That whether you are as a queen, waiting and watching as the Eagle lands, or the one inside the space suit whose foot first steps on unearthly virgin soil, doesn't matter. What is important is the possibility, the adventure, the spirit of exploration. The opening up of the human mind to acknowledge the infinite stretches, the immense sea that is the universe. The realization that the earth beneath our feet seems vast because we are so small.

One giant leap for mankind – a leap bigger than all our tiny footsteps put together and strung out like a ribbon circling the globe – that's how big this foot print, this first human mark on the moon, made the people feel. From Provincetown to Gloucester, Boston to Springfield and beyond, it was something for the whole world to see. An event that could only be taken in doses of humility and wonder.

Later that night, Glory thought about which way she'd take the meaning of the moon landing. For once, she wasn't sure. She felt humbled. She wanted to give credit where credit was due. She didn't know if she herself deserved any, what her life added up to. She didn't know what to believe, what could be true.

She looked out her bedroom window at the moon.

It's half hidden behind the big oak tree across the street in the field. I've never liked oaks — not quite sure why. The pines are gentler, but too soft to climb. And you can get lost in the pines.

The maples have their faults, too. You can climb high and hide in the limbs, but then their leaves fall off and you're exposed. And those pretentious leaves, so striking in red and gold, will stir up trouble at the first sign of a breeze.

Even so, the maples are better by far than the haughty overbearing oaks with their hard harsh barks. They think they'll live forever, they refuse to bend, but it only takes one good blow to topple them down. One decent wind.

There's no wind where Apollo 11 set foot, no atmosphere at all. If the moon had carbon dioxide, oaks could set their roots in lunar soil and have a perfect place to grow.

But why spoil the moon?

She couldn't sleep thinking about the damn trees and the moon. She needed to get past the trees, to see that circle of lunar soil fully parading by in all its glory. In all its majesty and mystery. She tiptoed around her bedpost, past Penny and stole out of her room.

Glory thought of waking Penny, but Penny was still upset about prom night, and wasn't talking with her sister. Penny had decided that college couldn't come fast enough for her. She'd leave and never come back, maybe not even for Thanksgiving. She'd eventually give in and talk with Glory, but she'd never trust her, never have a friendship with her again. Never seek her out.

I don't know all that Penny thinks of course, but I have a pretty good idea of it. If I were Penny, I'd be sick of this family too. I'd be tired of having to make do, of taking on all the responsibility as though I were the mother. I'd be worn out and resentful, just like Penny, and wanting desperately to get away.

You have to give Penny credit for all those times when she stepped in and saved us and took care of us. When she acted more a mother to us than our real one did. I guess I'll leave Penny be. Let her rest, knowing she'll work things out in her own way, in her own good time.

Gloria walked as quietly as she could through Sammy's room. She opened the creaky door to the bedroom where Kit, Suzi, and Davey slept. Then she pushed open the heavy door that led to the first attic in the house.

She climbed two sets of dusty, dirty stairs and landed all the way at the top of the house, in the very peak at the front of the roof. Looking out was a window with a clear view of the street and the field stretching behind it. It was a long straight drop to the yard below.

Through the cobwebbed panes, Glory looked past it all to see the magnificent moon. She rubbed the glass to get a better view.

It's worth the climb to have moon beams shining on me directly with no oak branches and no unhappy playing fields to mar the view. Simplicity itself, nothing complex, prime numbers only. The best that Mother Nature has to offer. No savages up here tonight. Not even within me.

She forced open the window.

To have the moon all to myself is supreme, so cool, so totally cool. Wicked cool, really. Moon beams are manna from heaven.

Glory gazed at the smoky haze that clouded around the moon.

I wonder if Neil Armstrong or Buzz Aldrin saw that haze as they were landing. Maybe only Michael Collins noticed it, because he stayed inside the command module and had to be content with witnessing events from above.

The great Elizabeth had to wait and watch too. It isn't easy to wait, perched on the edge of your throne or suspended in space, seeing others off on their promising adventures, knowing it's not your turn.

Follow the rules — it may never be your turn. Stay behind - you don't know what you've missed. Forge ahead to claim all the credit. But Michael Collins didn't seem to mind. Maybe he saw something just as special in that haze as the men who set foot on the moon. Maybe his story was just as worth the telling.

Glory leaned out the window. She hovered at the height of the house with its sheer cliff walls.

I wonder if my wait is over.

She looked down. The same dizziness that came to her in the stairwell from the time she branded her body overwhelmed her now. Her perch was as high as an eagle's.

What good is my life? What do I deserve?

She pondered that mysterious haze. Considered the dawn to come.

Aurora, will I see you again?

She reached for the moon, trying to discern the course Mother Nature had laid out for her.

Oh Moon, is it time?

Then in the darkness of the attic, she felt a sharp tap on her elbow.

Glory jumped.

She jumped, as they say, right out of her skin.

She shrieked to the heavens, loud enough to frighten even the mighty oaks below. In disorientation and fear, she turned to meet the savages before her.

There was Ma, standing and grinning at Glory as though she'd just played the joke of a lifetime on her. Ma laughed in hysterics at the look on her daughter's panicked face. "What in the world are you doing up here, my dear?" she asked after she had calmed down and was able to speak.

"What am *I* doing? I'm looking at the moon. What are you doing?" Glory couldn't believe the sight of Ma standing in her old grey nightgown and slippers. Her hair was pulled back in a loose messy bun. She was holding a slide rule, and a pencil and pad of paper.

"I'm taking measurements," Ma said simply. "You know Beth? Of course you know your friend Beth."

"What does Beth have to do with coming up to the attic?"

"Well you know her father is a professor at the teaching college. He teaches astronomy and physics – you knew that, right?" Glory didn't know, but she nodded like she did. Who knew anything about parents?

"He's been doing research over the past year on the subject of moon craters. He's studying them for a paper he's writing. I've been helping him to collect data, just a little, just as a supplement. I use a telescope he's loaned me and I take measurements. I use the slide rule to make calculations. And I take notes in this journal."

"You do?" Glory was bewildered, like she thought her mother was a little green man made of cheese.

Joyce sighed. Her daughter, quick in many ways, could be dense.

"I like helping him with his scientific research. You know, Glory, I never went to college but I always wish I had. There is so much to know, so much to find out about. So many possibilities if you let go of the past, if you open yourself up to the future. Do you want to see where I keep the telescope?"

Glory nodded. She was still in shock to see her mother appear, like a ghost in grey in the attic.

Ma opened the closet, the one that held Davey's cave paintings. She smiled as she shone her flashlight at the drawings. "That Davey," she said with respect. "Either he's going to be a great artist or a seriously troubled man, maybe both. Over time, I guess we'll find out."

She shined her light at the telescope. Glory stepped into the closet and looked with admiration at the instrument that made Ma happy in a way that her kids and husband couldn't, that got her out of bed and up from her books and cigarettes. That inspired her to believe in a new frontier, a better day.

She looked at the scope, and then saw something else behind it.

"Ma, what's this?" They moved the telescope out of its place and looked again into the closet. They pulled the object out.

It was a shovel, with a long wooden hand carved handle and a straight, blunt cut metal blade. On the wood was carved the initial "L." It was a curious thing to find way up high in their old attic.

"I recall, the last owners said that this house used to be an old potato farm," said Ma. "Before dairy farms came in, our town grew a lot of potatoes. This was the original house in the area, built way before the Civil War, before all the houses around us. I'll bet this is a potato shovel. Probably a hundred years old or more."

They looked out the window, together, at the unworldly beauty of the soft lit moon. God-lit, some might say, but not Joyce and not her daughter either. "The moon carries its own weight while revolving around the earth, and shines from the reflection of the sun," Ma observed. "It's a prime relationship, can't be reduced. There's nothing supernatural about it. It follows the laws of nature.

And now, even as we look, the moon has changed. It's grown by an infinitesimal amount because we are there. No instrument can measure the impact. But still, it's true, and amazing – humankind unafraid to try, to make a difference, to cast our steps and walk on the surface of the moon."

Joyce turned and looked squarely at her daughter, the girl with moon shine in her violet eyes.

"Gloria," she said quite seriously. "Don't let anyone stop you from being the best that you can be. Even yourself. Especially yourself. Because your best is good enough, Queen Glory the Extraordinary...the Lonely. The sun and the moon and the stars themselves demand no less from you. Not to mention your mother, of course. I know things haven't been easy, my dear. But no matter how difficult your journey, please, don't ever settle. No regrets, okay?"

I was surprised by how much my mother spoke, by how much she so obviously felt. Was she imparting another of life's great secrets?

I didn't know why Ma said what she did, why it seemed so important to her to tell me not to give up. They were Ma's feelings, and couldn't be denied. I hadn't thought of my mother as an actual person with real needs and desires and wants.

But there she was, not a steely glimmer or a grey specter of a person. Not an absent parent or a mother who didn't care. But a real, three dimensional, living, breathing, intelligent and philosophical and poetic woman, a thinking human being. Who knows me better than I know myself.

They propped up the shovel by the door. They'd bring it down in the morning. There might be someone else in the family who'd be interested in the history of their house.

Not that it was an earth shattering event like stepping onto the moon. Or life altering like carving fifteen signs of despair into your thighs and breasts and waiting for someone to notice. Or even massively relieving like realizing you're not psychotic, you're not going crazy or seeing grey ghosts.

It was a smaller history, a little event, finding that shovel in the light of a haze drawn moon. One small step for a girl. No giant leaps in sight.

But somehow, maybe it was a story worth telling.

POSTSCRIPT FROM AN ANCIENT GLORY

[from oceans away, across a sea of time]

Truth be told, my mother never discovered a way to be happy, never gave me the words of advice and affirmation in the attic under a hazy moon. The shovel was real, but the rest, I made up. I had a neurotic need for closure, some lunatic passion for a happier ending. Some fairy tale desire, nothing real.

Throughout the years, I remember her telling me life's great secrets.

"Most people are ugly."
"Life is hard."
"Life is unfair."

No follow up, no optimistic turn around, no comforting positive philosophy, not even a little. No sense that my life will be better, or even good enough, if I try my best to make it so.

Perhaps I have a bit of a real queen in me after all. Because I decided that I wanted to live. And I've learned something, not from all my imaginings and escapes, my fractured histories. But from the actions of my sister Penny — from Penny the Practical and the story of her prom.

I've learned there is nothing to be done but accept the explanations. Block out the pain. Go on. Even a queen can only wait so long for good news from across a wide ocean. At some point, she's got to move on.

So I've let it all go, forgiven Ma and Dad and yes, even Sammy for all their exceedingly human imperfections. For all the years of hurtful behavior, for lack of hugs, kisses or caring. For unseeing neglect. Because I don't think they meant it. I don't think they meant not to love us.

I'm the last one to give advice, me with my wicked long list of ugly insecurities and bad habits, my crazy thoughts and impulsive deeds. But I'll say it anyway, even to myself so maybe it will stick - here goes.

To Queen Glory and to Penny and Kit and Suzi, and Davey too though there's another story: Try to think they love you – they do, to give them credit, you know they do.

Live your life, even if it is the pits, even if it is at times cold and lonely and scary and uncool. Stay alive and watch out for the wind. But let moonlight and soft pines in, blueberries and corn on the cob; strawberries in summer, crisp apples in fall. Take comfort in the sound of the ocean in a shell. You're not too old to run after the ice cream truck, and the breadbox can be clean. It can be full with homemade fudge and devil's food cake now and again. There's cinnamon sugared bread for the making.

There's college, and Easy Bake Ovens, fairy dolls and wooden sleds and dogs named Duke. Remember Nannie, who cared for us all. And blue lights, the bluest of the blue to help you dream. Truth be told, even the goddess Persephone is happy, if only for half each year.

And scars will lighten, they'll pale unless you keep rubbing at them. Best to let them be, let them fade away in their own good time, in their own difficult and savage, cruelly dissonant way. Wait long enough, they'll fade – it's the law of nature.

Made in the USA
Lexington, KY
10 October 2014